When it comes to vampires and cowboys... *nobody* does it better than Kimberly Raye!

Dear Reader,

I've always been a hopeless romantic. The type that tears up during Mastercard commercials and openly weeps reading a Valentine's Day card. Cheesy, I know. But what can I say? I'm a firm believer in soul mates and love and all that mushy stuff. Deep in my heart, I just *know* that everyone has a certain special someone that they're meant to be with *forever*.

Big sigh...

I know reality doesn't pan out that way sometimes, but what if it did? It's this very question that gave me the idea for Garret's story, the third in my LOVE AT FIRST BITE series. Garret Sawyer—überhot cowboy and the hunkiest vampire in Skull Creek, Texas—met his soul mate, Viviana, years ago (we're talking a whopping two hundred), only to have her betray him. He's finally managed to put the past behind him. His custom motorcycle business is thriving. Even more, he's *this* close to finding and killing the Ancient Vampire who turned him. If he destroys his sire, he'll break the curse and free not only himself, but his two best friends. Garret is a vampire with one thing on his mind now and it certainly isn't Viviana Darland.

That is, until she shows up in Skull Creek...

Thanks for joining Garret and Viv as they live out their hottest fantasies and make peace with each other, and the past, in *A Body To Die For*. I hope you have as much fun reading their story as I did writing it. I love to hear from readers! You can visit me online at www.kimberlyraye.com or write to me c/o Harlequin Books, 225 Duncan Mill Road, Don Mills, Ontario M3B 3K9, Canada.

Much love from one hopeless romantic to another...

Kimberly Raye

KIMBERLY RAYE
A Body
To Die For

HARLEQUIN®

TORONTO • NEW YORK • LONDON
AMSTERDAM • PARIS • SYDNEY • HAMBURG
STOCKHOLM • ATHENS • TOKYO • MILAN • MADRID
PRAGUE • WARSAW • BUDAPEST • AUCKLAND

ISBN-13: 978-0-373-79435-5
ISBN-10: 0-373-79435-5

A BODY TO DIE FOR

This edition published by arrangement with Harlequin Books S.A.

® and TM are trademarks of the publisher. Trademarks indicated with ® are registered in the United States Patent and Trademark Office, the Canadian Trade Marks Office and in other countries.

www.eHarlequin.com

Printed in U.S.A.

ABOUT THE AUTHOR

Bestselling author Kimberly Raye started her first novel in high school and has been writing ever since. To date, she's published more than forty-five novels, two of them prestigious RITA® Award nominees. She's also been nominated by *Romantic Times BOOKreviews* for several Reviewers' Choice awards, as well as a career achievement award. Currently she is writing a romantic vampire mystery series for Ballantine Books that was recently optioned by ABC for a television series. She also writes steamy contemporary reads for Harlequin's Blaze line. Kim lives deep in the heart of the Texas Hill Country with her very own cowboy, Curt, and their young children. She's an avid reader who loves Diet Dr. Pepper, chocolate, Toby Keith, chocolate, alpha males (*especially* vampires) and chocolate. Kim also loves to hear from readers. You can visit her online at www.kimberlyraye.com.

Don't miss any of our special offers. Write to us at the following address for information on our newest releases.

Harlequin Reader Service
U.S.: 3010 Walden Ave., P.O. Box 1325, Buffalo, NY 14269
Canadian: P.O. Box 609, Fort Erie, Ont. L2A 5X3

For all of you hopeless romantics out there...
We rock!

1

HE SMELLED LIKE SEX.

Rich. Potent. Mesmerizing. Like a creamy dark truffle mousse with a drizzle of imported white chocolate, a dollop of whipped raspberry cream and a sprinkle of cinnamon-crusted pecans.

The crazy thought struck as she stood in the middle of The Iron Horseshoe—a rough and rowdy bar just off the interstate—and stared at the man who sat at a nearby table.

Crazy because Viviana Darland didn't normally think in terms of food.

She didn't do chocolate or whipped cream or pecans. She didn't do anything edible, period. She was a vampire who thrived on sex and blood, and so her thoughts rarely read like a transcript of the latest Rachael Ray episode.

But sheer desperation—coupled with the past two days spent holed up at the Skull Creek Inn, watching the Food Network and trying to work up her courage to approach Mr. Luscious and Edible—was new to her and so it only made sense that she would act out of character.

After all, her days were numbered.

A wild, rebellious southern rock song poured from the speakers and vibrated the air around her. Her heart beat faster, keeping tempo with the steady ba-bom ba-bom ba-bom of the drums. A neon Harley Davidson sign glowed above the bar and various motorcycle memorabilia— from studded leather chaps to an *Easy Rider* poster— decorated the walls.

Several truck drivers, their big rigs parked out back, sucked down a round of beers at a nearby table. A group of leather-clad bikers clustered around a dartboard in the far corner. A handful of men sporting long hair, beards and Golden Chopper Motorcycle Club jackets chugged Coronas at the massive bar that spanned the length of one wall.

The loud clack of pool balls echoed above the music. Cigarette smoke thickened the air. The sharp smell of Jack Daniels hovered around her.

It was a far cry from the latest "it" bar down in West Hollywood. She swallowed against a sudden lump in her throat.

So?

You're a vampire. You adapt to any place, any time, any situation. Stop making excuses, walk over and just tell him what you want.

The command echoed in her head and urged her forward. Unfortunately, her body didn't obey any more now than when she'd first spotted him a few days ago.

The memory rolled through her as she turned left and headed for the bar. She angled herself between two big bruisers and ordered a house beer.

She'd been on her way into the desperately small Texas town when she'd seen the hunky guy parked outside the city limits on the side of the highway. Wishful thinking, or so she'd thought.

But Garret Sawyer had been more than a figment of her imagination.

He'd been flesh and blood and oh, so real.

As real as the day she'd first met him. Touched him. Kissed him. Loved him.

Talk about opportunity. Forget tracking him down and arranging a chance meeting. She could dispense with formality and cut right to the chase.

At least that's what she'd told herself when she'd climbed out of her car and approached him.

But then she'd glimpsed the surprise in his gaze, the anger, the hurt and her resolve had crumbled. She'd barely managed a "Long time no see" before she'd hightailed it back to her car.

She hadn't seen him since.

But she'd asked around.

With Skull Creek being the quintessential small town, she'd gotten an earful from everyone—from the clerk at the Piggly Wiggly, to the fry guy at the Dairy Freeze.

She'd learned that Garret was the skill and expertise behind Skull Creek Choppers, the town's one and only custom motorcycle shop. He'd opened his doors a few months ago and bought a small ranch just outside the city limits. He had two business partners—Jake McCann handled the design and Dillon Cash monitored the software and computer system.

Garret bought coffee at the local diner every evening and subscribed to the *Skull Creek Gazette*. He also sponsored a local little league team, donated to the senior's center and served on the board of the Skull Creek Chamber of Commerce.

Exactly what she would have expected from a thirty-something businessman trying to establish himself in a new location.

Exactly what she wouldn't have expected from a two hundred-year-old vampire who'd always avoided hanging around too long in any one place.

"It's on me," the bruiser to the right said when she slid a five across the bar to pay for her drink.

Her head snapped up, and she found herself staring into a pair of interested brown eyes.

The man had long, black, greasy hair and a thick beard. He reeked of beer and cigarettes and sexual frustration. He missed his wife. But not because she'd been a fine upstanding woman who'd taken her vows seriously. No, she'd been the opposite. A slut who'd slept around on him every time he'd pulled out of town.

What he missed was having a warm body to turn to in the dead of night. He'd never been much of a player, and so he hadn't actually dated much before he'd met his missus. He wasn't even the type of man who offered to buy a woman a drink.

Until tonight.

Viv read the truth in his eyes and felt his desperation. And suddenly it didn't matter that he wasn't the most attractive man she'd ever met. All that mattered was the sexual energy bubbling inside of him.

The desire.

The need.

Her own hunger stirred, reminding her just how long it had been since she'd fed. Her chest tightened, and her stomach hollowed out. Her hands trembled, and it took all of her strength not to reach out and take the man up on his blatant offer.

But this wasn't about getting a quick fix and fulfilling some stranger's fantasies.

This was about fulfilling her own.

"Thanks, but no thanks." But you might try with the blonde over there in the corner, she added silently. I think she likes you.

He fixated on Viv for a few long moments before the message seemed to penetrate. Finally, his eyes sparked, and hope fired to life inside of him. He turned toward the woman who sat nearby, nursing a margarita and eyeballing him.

Viv took her beer and shifted her attention back to the real reason she'd come to the Iron Horseshoe in the first place.

He sat facing her, his back to the wall, his feet propped on the table in front of him. He wore faded jeans that outlined his trim waist and muscular thighs. A frayed black T-shirt, the words Easy Rider emblazoned in neon blue and silver script, hugged his broad chest and sinewy biceps. Black gloves, the fingers cut out, accented his large hands. A tiny silver skull dangled from one ear. The only thing about him that didn't scream bad-ass biker was the black Stetson sitting on the table near his beer and the black cowboy boots that covered his feet.

She eyed the scuffed toes of the boots before dragging her gaze back up, over his long legs, the hard, lean lines of his torso, the tanned column of his throat.

Her attention stalled on the faint throb of his pulse, and her mouth went dry. Despite the crying guitar and pounding drums, she could hear the steady pump of his heart. The sound called to her, inviting her closer, while fear held her stiff.

Her fingers flexed on the ice-cold bottle of beer. Her gaze stalled on his face, and she licked her suddenly dry lips.

He had short, cropped brown hair and the rugged features of a man who'd spent more than one day in the saddle. A day's growth of stubble darkened his jaw and outlined his sensuous lips. Pale blue eyes collided with hers.

There was no flicker of surprise, no glimmer of pain. Just pure, unadulterated lust.

As if he'd been waiting for her, wanting her, as much as she'd been wanting him.

A fierce longing knifed through her, and for the first time in a very long time—one hundred and eighty years to be exact—she felt her legs tremble.

The reaction fortified her courage. It also erased any lingering doubts about her decision to leave L.A. and her freelance career as a tabloid photographer, for a small Texas town and an assignment with a regional travel magazine.

She'd ditched it all for sex.

For him.

Because Garret Sawyer had been the first man to give her a mind-blowing orgasm.

The only man.

And Viviana Darland wanted one more before her past finally caught up with her, and she bit the dust for good.

HE HAD TO BE DREAMING.

Another full-blown, heart-stopping, aching hard-on fantasy.

Because no way—no friggin' way—was she really here.

Right here.

Right now.

She eased off the bar stool and stepped toward him, and reality sank in.

Shit.

That's what his head said. But his damned traitorous body wasn't nearly as pissed.

His muscles tightened. His spine stiffened. Heat swept through him, firebombing his dick until it throbbed to full awareness. His eyes drank in the sight of her, roving from her head to her red-tipped toes and back up again just as she reached his table.

She looked different now. So damned different.

Instead of being pulled back, her long black hair

hung in soft waves around her face, accenting her bright blue eyes and full pink lips. A fitted navy blue jacket molded to her lush breasts and tiny waist. A matching skirt outlined her curvaceous hips. High-heeled sandals made her legs seem that much longer than the full skirts and petticoats she'd worn way back when.

Different, yet she still had the same glimmer in her eyes. The same confidence in her stance.

His nostrils flared, and he drank in the same warm scent of apples and cinnamon that he remembered so well.

"Is this seat taken?" Her soft, familiar voice slid into his ears and jump-started his heart. Before he could reply, she pulled out the chair opposite him and folded herself into it.

The music blared a fast ZZ Top song that kept time with his racing pulse. "What are you doing here?" he finally asked after a long, loud moment.

She held up a bottle of Lonestar and gave him the faintest smile. "Thought I'd sample some of the local brew."

"Not here at the Horseshoe." His gaze narrowed, colliding with hers. "Here. This town."

She shrugged. "I'm on assignment."

That's what she said. But her eyes. Those bluer-than-blue eyes said something much different. He didn't miss the flash of desperation. Or the glimmer of need.

"We haven't had any alien abductions or Elvis sightings in a while," he said, sarcastically.

"I'm not working for *The Gossip Guru* anymore," she said, referring to the national tabloid that sat next to the cash register at every grocery store and gas station in town. "I'm freelancing now. I'm doing a travel article on small towns." Her gaze collided with his. "Sexy small towns."

Her words stirred a rush of memories he'd buried a long, long time ago. Memories of the two of them having wild and crazy—

Garret hit the brakes and made a U-turn before he wasted another second going down the wrong road.

He'd traveled that path once before, and he'd crashed and burned in a major way. Sure, he couldn't help a wet dream every now and then. But that was pure fantasy. An escape from the monotony of living year after year after year.

He sure as hell wasn't stupid enough to go for the real thing.

Not ever again.

He leaned back in his chair and folded his arms. "It's dusty here. And hot. And it smells like cow shit when the wind blows due south. We're smack dab in the middle of ranch country. There's nothing sexy about it."

"Not to you because you live here. But if you were stuck in New York or Chicago or Detroit, it would be a different story. There are quite a few people who would love to escape the daily grind of civilization and get back to nature. In a small town, you can do that. There's no traffic congestion. No pollution fogging the air. No concrete jungle. Just lots of birds and trees and rolling countryside." She smiled. "Come on, you have to admit the view around here is pretty incredible."

Damn straight.

She paused to lick her lips, and he couldn't help but follow the motion with his gaze.

His stomach did a one-eighty, and the words were out before he could stop himself. "I suppose it's nice enough. But sexy?"

"It can be. If you're with that special someone. There are couples all over the world eager to find an old, quaint small town with friendly people and lots of local color for a romantic getaway."

"You've just described every town from here to the Rio Grande. That still doesn't answer my question— why this particular town?" My town? His gaze collided with hers and he found himself wishing he could read her thoughts the way he could read those of humans.

But she was a vampire.

She always had been.

A knife twisted in his gut, and he stiffened. "Why Skull Creek?" he pressed.

She didn't say anything for a long moment. Instead, she licked her lips again. Once. Twice. If he hadn't known better, he would have sworn she was trying to work up her courage.

But he knew better.

Viv had never come up short on courage. She was a bloodsucker who took what she wanted. And discarded what she didn't want.

He knew that firsthand.

"Why not Skull Creek?" she countered. "Besides, it's not the only town I'm featuring. Just one of five I'm visiting for this particular article." The music closed in on them for several long seconds as Bob Seger launched into "Night Moves."

"A travel piece, huh?" he finally said. "Sounds tame compared to the stuff you're used to."

She shrugged and took a swig of her beer. "I was due for a change of pace."

"And here I thought you'd come all this way to see me."

"Actually…" Her voice faded as she seemed to search for her next words. "I did." Her gaze locked with his, and he saw it again—the flash of desperation, along with a glimmer of fear. "I…" She swallowed. "That, is, I know you recently opened a motorcycle shop in town, and I thought maybe I could take a few pictures for my article. You know, to showcase all that Skull Creek has to offer. I've taken shots of Mr. McClury's jasmine fields and the gazebo in the town square. I know a motorcycle shop doesn't seem all that sexy, but it's the implication. Two lovebirds riding off into the sunset." When he didn't say anything, she added, "It's just a few pictures. You won't have to do anything. Just be there to let me in and out and answer a few questions."

"What's in it for me?"

"Free promotion. In exchange for the photos, the magazine will mention your contact information and even give you a free half page ad." She smiled and he had the sudden urge to get the hell out of there while the getting was good.

The last thing he needed was to let Viviana back into his life, even for a measly travel article. He'd had a hard enough time putting the past behind him.

Better to keep his distance and his sanity.

At the same time, he couldn't stifle the voice that told him there was something up besides his traitorous cock.

She wanted more from him than a few pictures, and he couldn't shake the sudden urge to find out exactly how much.

No way did he want to spend any time with her because he still had feelings for her. Anything he'd once felt had died a long time ago, right along with his humanity. The only thing left now was the lust that lived and breathed inside of him. And that, he felt for every woman.

A lust he'd been denying since he'd moved to Skull Creek. He was tired of the endless one-night stands. Even more, he was tired of being a vampire.

He wanted out.

He wanted his humanity back.

"I'm busy with a project right now—a custom chopper we've designed for some bigwig up in Dallas. You'll have to stay out of the way."

She nodded. "No problem. You won't even know I'm there."

He sucked down the last of his drink. "Tomorrow night then. Seven o'clock."

Excitement lit her expression as she got to her feet. "It's a date."

If only.

He squelched the thought, sipped his beer and watched the push/pull of her denim skirt as she turned to walk away.

Watch being the key word. A word that implied distance and perspective and hands off.

But looking…

Well, there wasn't a damned thing wrong with that.

2

EVERY INCH of Viv's body screamed with awareness as she left Garret staring after her and headed for the nearest exit.

Her hands trembled. Her stomach tingled. Her nipples quivered. Heat flamed her cheeks, and she felt a buzzing awareness from her hair follicles to the balls of her feet. The chemistry between them was even stronger than she'd remembered.

Which explained why she'd chickened out with her real proposition.

She wanted a lot of things from Garret Sawyer—his hands on her skin, his lips eating at hers and his body full and thick inside of her—but a picture wasn't one of them.

Unless said picture included all of the above.

But still shots of his motorcycle shop?

Forget desperate. One hundred and eighty years without an orgasm had finally taken its toll. She'd crossed the line from desperate to completely deranged.

"Hey there, sweet thing."

Her gaze snapped up just as a man stepped in front

of her and blocked her escape route. It was one of the bikers who'd been playing darts when she'd first entered the bar.

He slid his arm around her shoulder and leaned into her. "Why don't you and I have a seat and get to know each other better?"

That's what he said, but she knew the truth. He didn't want to get to know her. Not her mind, that is. As for having a seat… The only seat he had in mind involved her straddling his lap and doing her best rodeo queen imitation.

"No, thanks."

"Aw, don't be like that." His thick fingers stroked her arm. "I just want to be friends."

"I doubt that." Garret's deep voice drifted over her shoulder and prickled the hair on the back of her neck.

The man turned and his eyes went wide. "Where'd you come from?"

"Do you really want to know?"

The man blinked and shook his head. "Weren't you just sitting clear across the room?"

"I've got fast reflexes." When the man didn't look convinced, Garret added, "Shouldn't you be at home with Liza?"

Shock fueled the man's expression and his gaze narrowed. "What do you know about my wife?"

"I know she left your sorry ass because you've got a hair trigger when it comes to sex. I also know that the two of you are still married even though she's staying at her mother's." Garret's expression was as hard as granite. "You shouldn't be here hitting on women. You should be begging Liza's forgiveness."

The man looked confused for a long moment before an idea seemed to strike. "You're one of them super-heroes, ain't ya?"

"Not even close," Garret replied.

"What about a psychic? My Aunt Bertie was a psychic. She had forty cats and swore she could talk to every one of them. Always knew when one was getting sick."

"I'm not psychic either. I'm pissed. So get your hands off the lady. Now."

"Like hell—" he started, but his voice faded when Garret's gaze collided with his.

"Go home," Garret told the man.

And beg your wife to take you back. Viv added the silent thought when the man's gaze finally shifted to hers. He nodded and released her arm.

"Thanks," she told Garret when the man finally walked away. "But you didn't have to do that. I can take care of myself."

"I know." His gaze drilled into hers, and for a split second time pulled her back, and the wall between them seemed to crumble.

Concern sparkled in his eyes, along with a fierce protective light that stalled her heart.

"About those pictures," she heard herself say. "I…" *I was lying. I don't want to take your picture. I want you. Wild and naked and inside of me.* She opened her mouth, but despite the moment of déjà vu, she couldn't seem to force the words past her lips. "I—I can't wait to get started," she heard herself say. "See you tomorrow." And then she turned and pushed through the Exit door.

The sweltering Texas night sucked her up, and the door rocked shut behind her. Gravel crunched as she headed for the silver Jag parked at the far end of a row of motorcycles. Her ears tuned for any sound that would indicate that Garret followed.

Nothing.

A wave of disappointment crashed through her, followed by a surge of relief.

Relief? What the hell was wrong with her?

She should have hauled him outside with her, shoved him up against the nearest wall, kissed him full on the mouth and made her intentions crystal clear.

That's what she would have done with anybody else. What she'd always done to keep up her strength and feed the hunger that churned deep inside her.

But while she'd soaked up plenty of sexual energy from her partner's orgasms, she'd never closed her eyes and lost herself in the feel of her own body convulsing and splintering into a thousand little pieces.

Not since her last night with Garret.

She'd been a vampire back then and he'd been just another mortal, but the encounter had rocked her unlike any other. They'd had phenomenal sex and she'd been hooked.

And so had he.

The crazy fool had actually proposed to her.

She touched her bare ring finger. She could still feel the metal sliding over her knuckle. In her mind's eye, she saw the ornate gold band and the bloodred princess-cut ruby. It had been small. Very small but pretty. His grandmother's, he'd told her.

She'd smiled indulgently and played along for a while. The way she always did when it came to men.

She was a vampire. Charismatic. Mesmerizing. She could be dressed in baggy sweats, having the worst hair day on the planet, and men would still find her irresistible. It hadn't been a bit surprising that Garret had fallen so hard for her so fast.

No, what had really startled her was what she'd felt for him.

She'd actually liked him.

He'd been a patriot of Texas. Strong. Noble. Courageous. And from the moment he'd walked into the small saloon where she'd been working, aka feeding, she'd been attracted.

So she'd done the unthinkable—she'd slept with him not once but several times. Even more than the sex, they'd actually spent time together.

They'd gone on moonlit walks, held hands beneath the stars and confided their dreams to each other.

Wild, far-out dreams of love and marriage and kids and a real home.

She'd been a newly turned vampire back then, desperate to ignore the truth of what she'd become. Likewise, he'd been a man eager to escape the death and destruction that lived and breathed all around him.

And so she'd pretended, and he'd pretended.

She'd seen the love swimming in his eyes, and she'd let herself believe it was real.

But it hadn't been.

Not then and certainly not now.

He was no longer a weak human mesmerized by her vampiric charm, and she was no longer denying her true nature.

They were both vampires, fully rooted in the present. When they had sex again, there would be no soft words between them, no foolhardy talk of happily ever after. No false promises.

Just lust.

Raw.

Primitive.

Savage.

If they came together.

The doubt pushed its way into her head as she climbed behind the wheel of her car and keyed the ignition.

There could be no if.

Sex had to be a sure thing, and the lame excuse she'd given him tonight would work in her favor. Pictures meant more than one. Which meant they wouldn't be spending five minutes together sharing small talk. It would take hours, maybe even days, for her to set up her equipment—the cameras, the lighting, the background—and get just the right shots. She had no doubt that the more time they spent with one another, the more explosive the chemistry would be.

Because he wanted her as fiercely as she wanted him.

Even though she could no longer stare into his eyes and see his every thought—vamps couldn't read other vamps the way they did humans—she'd seen the telltale spark in his gaze when she'd sat down at his table. She'd felt the rush of jealousy when he'd come to her rescue.

Something was bound to happen between them.

Eventually.

Before Cruz and Molly caught up with her again?

The question struck, and her survival instincts kicked into gear. She swept a glance around her, drinking in the half-full parking lot. Her gaze sliced through the darkness, pushing back the shadows, searching. Her ears perked, and her nostrils flared, but she smelled nothing except stale beer and cigarettes and her grip eased on the steering wheel.

She was safe. She knew it. She felt it.

For now.

Over the past year, it had taken at least a week or two for the other vampires to track her down once she'd given them the slip.

With the exception of their last encounter, that is.

When they'd left her for dead.

She'd been sensationalizing the latest in a string of serial murders in state courtesy of the Butcher.

The Butcher had eluded police over twenty-nine murders, and he was still on the loose. While true crime wasn't usually something picked up by a tabloid, the Butcher was the exception because he was rumored to be a Hollywood celebrity gone bad. At least that's what he'd told the world when he'd left a bloody message on the wall of his first victim's apartment. Every tabloid was now hot on the trail to discovery his identity first. Viv had been covering his handiwork from the beginning, from his first kill down in West Hollywood, to an elderly couple in Portland, to the recent handful of bodies found in an abandoned cabin outside of Tacoma.

She'd been scoping out the actual crime scene when she'd been discovered by local law enforcement, specifically a hard-ass sheriff by the name of Matt Keller. Keller had been about to grill her with questions—who did she work for, how did she hear about the murders, why was she there—when he'd been called back to the police station. He'd threatened to throw her ass in jail for trespassing and then he'd escorted her off the property. His parting words? "Stay the hell away from here."

She should have listened to him.

Instead, she'd gone back. She'd been snapping pictures when she'd been attacked by the two vampires who'd been hot on her trail for over three years. They'd staked her out on the front porch of the cabin and left her to fry.

But Molly's aim had been off. The knife had punctured her at an angle, a scant half-inch to the right. Rather than hitting her heart, they'd stabbed the inner right lobe of her lung. While not life-threatening, she'd still been hurt badly. She'd bled all over the porch, her blood mingling with that of the Butcher's other victims. She would have burned to a crisp at the first sign of dawn if she hadn't managed to drag herself through the front door. Inside, she'd hidden in one of the closets.

It was there, as she'd cowered beneath a mound of stale clothes, her St. Benedict medal clutched tightly in her hand, that she'd felt vulnerable for the first time in her life. Hurt. Nervous. Scared.

Cruz and Molly wanted their humanity back and they would stop at nothing in their quest to destroy the vampire who'd taken it from them.

She could still see their faces, the first time she'd met them all those years ago. Eighty-seven to be exact. She'd been in some hole-in-the-wall border town looking for her next meal when she'd happened upon a white slavery ring holed up in a house on the outskirts of town.

Molly had been chained in the cellar and Cruz had been one of her abductors. He'd fallen in love with her and tried to help her escape, and so he'd ended up chained next to her.

After a violent encounter with the one guard on duty (the rest of the slave traders had been upstairs passed out from a case of tequila), Viv had freed a cellar full of prisoners made up of primarily women and children.

Most of the prisoners had taken off up the rickety steps, desperate to get away before their abductors sobered up.

Except for Cruz and Molly.

They'd seen the truth about Viv, and they'd wanted a different means of escape.

The voices echoed in her head, so strong and clear, as if it had been just yesterday that she'd descended into that hell-hole prison.

"YOU CAN'T JUST leave us." Cruz held Molly's hand in one of his and a buck knife he'd taken off the guard in his other.

The man's body slumped in a nearby corner. He was out cold. For now.

"They'll track us down," Cruz went on. "They will." He nodded frantically. His eyes glittered with the horrific memories of being beaten and locked up and humiliated. He'd watched the woman he loved being raped. Over and over. And he'd been powerless to stop it.

He still was.

The truth burned inside of him, feeding the desperation and fear coiling his body tight.

"You have to help us," he added, his gaze as pleading as his words.

"Leave now," Viv told him. She couldn't do what he asked. She wouldn't doom anyone else to the darkness. Never again.

"You'll have a good head start," Viv continued. "Take Molly and go. I'll stall them for you."

"Kill them?"

But she couldn't do that either. While she'd made her fair share of vampires, she'd never actually caused anyone's death. No, she'd saved them from it.

Or so she'd always thought.

"I can't do that." She shook her head. "But I'll slow them down. That's all I can do."

"It won't be enough," came Molly's small, hollow voice. She shook her head, her eyes wide and vacant, as if the men had stolen her spirit right along with her innocence. "They'll find us."

"They won't," Viv reassured them. "But you have to go." She motioned toward the rickety steps leading to the dark, cold night. "Now."

"You don't know them." Cruz shook his head, a strange look in his eyes. He let go of Molly's hand and lifted the knife. "They'll catch us and make us pay. And I won't be able to stop them. I can't. Not like this."

The blade flashed and before Viv could blink, he sliced through his left wrist clear to the bone. Blood gushed, spurting out onto the floor at an alarming rate.

"Please," he mouthed, and then he sank to his knees as his life slipped away.

Viv blinked against the sudden burning in her eyes at the vivid memory. She hadn't been able to stand by and watch him die. Not after the suffering he'd already endured. And so she'd turned him.

And he'd turned Molly.

And then the two newly made vampires had doled out revenge.

But what they'd first seen as their salvation, they'd come to realize was more a curse.

One they now meant to break.

They'd finally figured out that if they killed her, they

could free themselves from the chains of darkness that bound them, silence the hunger that ruled their existence and become human again.

It had been eight days since Viviana had crawled into that closet and faced her mortality. She had no doubt that Cruz and Molly knew that they'd failed by now.

They would come for her again. To do the job right this time. And she would let them.

Because along with fear, she'd felt something else, as well, while she'd been holed up in that closet. As her body had healed, her mind had relived the past. She'd spent three days hiding, healing and thinking about her life, about all those people she'd tried to save from death.

She'd finally admitted the truth to herself—despite her intentions, she hadn't really saved anyone. No, she'd doomed them to a fate worse than death.

The darkness.

The hunger.

No more.

She figured she only had a few days before Molly and Cruz caught up with her again. When they did, she had no intention of fighting them. Rather, she would face her mistakes this time, and set things right. She would give them back their humanity.

But before she submitted to her own death, she wanted to feel truly alive one more time.

One last time.

She retrieved the medallion she'd left hanging from

the rearview mirror, slid the gold chain over her head and tucked the warm metal deep in her cleavage. Gunning the engine, she put the car in gear and headed back to the motel.

3

SHE WAS PERFECT.

Garret watched the redhead make her way across the sawdust floor. His nostrils flared. The faint scent of strawberry shampoo drifted through the fog of beer and cigarette smoke. Her breaths came quick, her lips parting ever so slightly. Her small breasts bounced with each draw of oxygen.

It had been an hour since Viv had left the bar.

An hour spent thinking and wondering and fantasizing.

He drop-kicked the last thought as soon as it waltzed into his head and focused on the hunger gnawing at his gut. His stomach clenched, and his muscles bunched. Heat clawed low and deep. His throat tightened.

His gaze narrowed, and he fixated on the woman again. He noticed everything about her—from the way her eyes glittered with excitement and fear to the slight sway of her walk, as if she hadn't pulled out the high heels in a really long time.

And then he noticed that no one else seemed to notice her.

The other men didn't stare or drool or eat her up with their eyes the way they'd done Viv.

Because there was nothing supernatural about this woman.

She was real.

Ordinary.

And so the men kept drinking and shooting the shit while the woman slid onto a bar stool and crossed her legs.

As if she felt his attention, she turned. Her green gaze collided with his, and the truth echoed in his head.

This was the last place she wanted to be, but she was sick and tired of sitting home alone, mourning over a recent break-up with her long-term boyfriend. She needed to ease her sexual frustration, get over him once and for all and get on with her life.

She needed rebound sex.

And Garret needed the energy bubbling inside of her, especially now that Viv was back in his life. If he meant to keep his head on straight and his dick in his pants, he needed every ounce of strength when he faced her tomorrow night.

He needed to suppress the hunger.

Satisfy it.

He pushed to his feet despite the promise he'd made to himself to give up the endless string of one-night stands that came with being a vampire. The constant need for blood and sex. The blood he couldn't deny himself. He'd been bagging it, courtesy of a contact he'd made at the Austin Blood Bank. But the sex… He wasn't going to sleep his way through Skull Creek the way he'd done every other town. He was tired of moving from place to place. Running. Existing. He wanted to live again.

He wanted his humanity back.

He could have it, too. It was just a matter of finding and destroying the vampire who'd turned him.

A nearly impossible task or so he'd thought. Until Dillon Cash—the computer genius behind Skull Creek Choppers—had come through with a solid lead.

It had started with a cheesy blog Dillon had started a few months ago to locate Garret's sire. Surprisingly enough, the blog had gained popularity. People had started to comment.

While the majority of visitors were vampire wannabes, there were a few legitimate posts. Enough for Dillon to come up with a lead on the vampire who fit the description in Garret's memory.

He didn't remember much. Just a dark, looming shadow, a sweet, succulent scent, and a gold medallion.

He'd sketched the medallion, and Dillon had blogged about it and now they had a name.

One that might lead him absolutely nowhere.

At the same time, there was a chance—however slim—that Garret might find himself that much closer to the Ancient One.

He'd hired a private investigator to track down the name. Dalton MacGregor, the decorated Green Beret and ex-cop who'd taken the case, had promised to have an address by the end of this week. Reason enough for

Garret to ignore the hunger churning inside of him and head for the door instead of the woman.

Five steps, and he reached her. Desire sparked in her gaze, and she licked her lips. A wave of self-consciousness swept through her, and she stiffened. She damned herself for not wearing the pink tank top instead of the white. White always made her look so flat-chested.

He dropped his gaze and let it linger on her cotton-clad breasts for a brief moment.

Nice. He sent the silent message and shifted his attention to her face in time to see her smile.

"What are you drinking?" he asked.

"Corona." She licked her lips again, and her heartbeat kicked up a notch.

The fast rhythm of it echoed in his head, and his gut tightened. He could see the faint pulse of blue at the base of her neck, and a knife twisted inside of him. He signaled the bartender to bring her a beer and ordered a shot of Jack Daniels for himself.

A few seconds later, the bartender deposited a frosty beer mug in front of the redhead and a shot glass in front of Garret. The man poured two fingers of fiery liquid before setting the whiskey bottle aside and rushing toward the opposite end of the bar to fill another request.

"Thanks," she said as she took a tentative sip from her mug. "So, um, do you come here often?"

"Every now and then."

"That's nice." She nodded and took another sip. "I've never been here myself, but I've always wanted to give it a try." She glanced around. "It's a little noisier than I expected. Not really ideal for getting to know some-one." She shifted her gaze back to his, suddenly eager to cut right to the chase now that she'd worked up her courage. "Maybe we could, um, go someplace quiet. That is, if you want." She took another sip.

Her red lipstick left an imprint on the frosted mug. The sight stirred a rush of memories, and just like that he was back in the Texas Star saloon with his regiment.

A drink.

That's all he'd wanted at first, but then he'd seen Viv Darland standing near the bar, and suddenly alcohol hadn't been enough.

He'd wanted her warm skin beneath his hands, her legs wrapped around his waist, her mouth soft and open beneath his own. He'd followed her upstairs, and he hadn't come down for days. He'd ended up staying so long he'd almost been declared AWOL by his com-manding officer.

Not that he'd cared.

Everything else—his family, his passion, his duty—had ceased to exist when he'd stared into Viv's blue eyes. He'd been hooked. Infatuated. Mesmerized.

Because she was a vampire.

He hadn't known then.

Sure, he'd seen the signs.

Her usually blue eyes had seemed purple at times, green at other times. She'd been stronger than most women, uncorking her own whiskey bottles and dealing with drunken brawlers all by herself. And, of course, her aversion to sunlight. But she'd been a saloon whore, plying her trade all night and sleeping all day, and so he hadn't thought much about it.

He'd fallen hard and fast, and he hadn't been able to pick himself back up. Hell, he hadn't wanted to.

She'd been the first thing he'd thought of when he'd opened his eyes every morning and the last thing when he'd closed them at night.

He'd even imagined her there at the end, leaning over him as he'd sprawled facedown on the ground, his blood seeping out into the dirt. Her scent had filled his head. Her soft, silky hair had brushed his temple. And just like that, he'd been distracted from the pain and suffering of the knife wounds.

A hallucination, of course.

He'd been miles away from the saloon when he'd been attacked by a group of Mexican bandits, robbed and left for dead.

An easy target for the vampire who'd come along to finish the job.

He could still remember the presence looming over his wounded body, the strong hand gripping his hair and yanking his head back, the razor-sharp fangs piercing his throat.

One minute he'd been hanging onto his life by a thread and the next, the line had snapped. Death had taken him, only to spit him back out when the vampire had rolled him over and drip-dropped his own blood into Garret's mouth.

Garret hadn't even caught a glimpse of his sire.

He'd been too weak to see more than a shadow looming over him.

Seconds later, he'd been alone, sprawled on the ground without a clue as to what had just happened. Until daybreak arrived and the first rays of sunlight topped the horizon.

The past pushed and pulled, snatching him from the here and now and luring him back to the morning of his turning.

He fought against the pain gripping him and forced his eyes open. He felt cold. So cold. His teeth chattered, and his body shook. He stared through blurry eyes. Orange topped the trees, promising warmth and a rush of relief went through him. Now he would warm up.

In…just…a…few…seconds…

A shaft of light fell across his face, and pain sliced clear to his bones. A hiss worked its way up his throat as he jerked his head to the side. The heat slashed across his shoulders, and he scrambled away. He staggered to his feet. Pain beat at his temples as the light cracked at his body like a red hot whip.

He stumbled for the trees, but they weren't enough to shield him completely. His skin burned and sizzled and he moved deeper into the forest. Light filtered down through the branches, stabbing him at every step. The pungent scent of charred flesh clogged his nostrils and choked him. Smoke burned his eyes, blurring his vision as he glanced around, frantic for a place to hide.

Another shaft of light broke through the trees, and he dodged to the left. His foot came up against a rock and he pitched forward, landing facedown on the ground. Clawing at the ground, he pushed until he managed to lift his head. A black hole loomed in front of him.

He dug his fingers into the dirt and pulled himself forward, over sharp rocks and prickly cactus until he managed to crawl inside. He went deeper, deeper, until the light disappeared and he found himself sheltered in the dark, cool interior.

Heaven.

That's what Garret had thought. The deep, narrow cave had been his shelter. His salvation.

But over the next several hours as the hunger had taken full control, the small space had turned into his own personal hell, a place where he'd fought a losing battle for his soul.

It was a battle that had lasted several days, as Garret remained hidden away in the cave, resisting the blood-lust and trying to come to terms with what he'd become.

Meanwhile, Viv had been back at the saloon, seducing any and every cowboy who'd walked in. Talking them into drinks. Luring them back to her room. Spreading her legs and opening her arms.

Deceiving them the way she'd deceived him.

The realization had come when he'd finally given in to the hunger and left the cave. He'd gone back to town in search of food. But before he'd sank his fangs into anyone, he'd gone to the saloon first. He'd meant to explain things to her, to beg for her help and her understanding.

But she'd already understood because she was every bit the vampire he'd become.

Even so, he'd thought that she still felt something for him. Something that went beyond the bloodlust and the need for sex.

Love.

He'd been wrong.

"I can't be with you like this. Not now. Not ever again."

He could still hear her voice as she'd turned her back and walked away from him.

She'd left him because he'd become a vampire who could see through her lies. A vampire who could no longer give her the sustenance she needed—the sexual energy—because he needed it for himself.

And so she'd abandoned him to find someone else to feed the beast that lived and breathed inside of her.

As for love… She hadn't loved him, and he hadn't really loved her. He'd been mesmerized by her, seduced by her vamp magic like any other weak human.

But he wasn't susceptible to her now.

Even if he did have an aching hard-on.

"What do you say?" The soft voice pushed into his thoughts and pulled him back to the present. To the smoke-filled bar and the horny woman sitting next to him. "Would you, um, like to come back to my place?"

Yes.

The answer was there on the tip of his tongue despite his self-made vow. He needed her. To ease the pain inside his body, feed the hunger and fill him with a burst of energy.

He felt so tired at that moment.

So damned hungry.

His gaze hooked on the lipstick imprint on her glass again, and his chest tightened. "I'm afraid I'm a little busy right now." He slid several bills onto the counter and reached for the bottle of Jack Daniels. "But you have a nice night, sugar." He turned and left her staring longingly after him.

Because even more than Garret Sawyer needed to feed, suddenly he needed to forget.

The dark hair.

The true blue eyes.

The luscious body and fragrant skin.

The damned voice that echoed over and over in his head "I can't be with you like this."

And so he sank down at the nearest table, touched the open bottle to his lips and did what he hadn't done since Viv Darland had walked out on him all those years ago.

He started to drink.

And he didn't stop.

4

"How's this?"

"Move a little to the right," Viv told the short, balding, forty-six-year-old man who stood behind the counter of Skull Creek's one and only motel.

It was two hours since she'd left the Iron Horseshoe, and she was desperate for a distraction. Something to pass the time and get her mind off Garret and the anticipation bubbling inside of her.

Enter Eldin Atkins.

He was the owner of the Skull Creek Inn and, more importantly, the oldest bachelor in town. He'd inherited both the motel and his grandmother, Winona, when his parents had retired to a small fishing port on the Gulf Coast. Eldin made all the reservations and looked after Winona while she puttered around, straightening rooms and poking her nose in everyone's business.

Or so Viv had heard from the waitress over at the diner.

Since Winona did most of her nosing around during the day when Viv had her door barricaded and her shades drawn, she'd yet to run into the old woman.

Eldin was a different story altogether.

The minute Viv had mentioned that she was a photo journalist, he'd gone above and beyond the call of duty to make her stay as memorable as possible.

He'd brought fresh towels every morning and had even upgraded her room for free. She now occupied the one and only deluxe suite with a full-size bathroom and a kitchenette.

Not that she needed the latter, but Eldin didn't know that. He was just out to attract as much attention as possible because he'd already tried every on-line dating service in the free world, and he still hadn't had any luck with the opposite sex.

He was hoping like hell that some poor, lonely female read the travel article, saw his picture and realized that, despite his thinning hair, introverted personality and live-in grandmother, he was a halfway decent catch.

He didn't wear women's underwear (not since Double Dog Dare Ya night back in the tenth grade) and he didn't suck his teeth and—and this was the biggee— he had his own business.

Sort of.

Technically, his parents still owned the place, but once they kicked the bucket, the Inn would be Eldin's free and clear.

Well, his and Winona's, but his grammy was already older than dirt, so how much longer could she actually last?

Bottom line, he wasn't such a bad guy. The article

would be a prime opportunity to show the single women of the southwest (and a few east coast states where the travel mag had been picked up) all that he had to offer.

Tonight he wore an orange Hawaiian-print shirt, beige walking shorts and a pair of tan boat shoes with tube socks. He had a king-sized Snickers bar in his left shirt pocket and a Slim Jim in the right.

"You're going to put my e-mail address in the article, right?" he asked. "Just in case somebody is of a mind to reach me? For a room, that is."

Or, more importantly, a date.

"E-mail and snail mail," Viv promised. "Say cheese."

"Wait a second." Eldin slicked his eyebrows down, threw his shoulders back and puffed out his chest. One hand paused on the wall of room keys and the other gave a little salute. "Okay, I'm ready."

"So, Eldin," Viv said as she checked the shutter on her camera, "do you always stand that way when you're checking someone in?"

He seemed to think before letting out a deep breath. "'Course not." He switched angles and struck the same pose. "I usually stand like this on account of it's my good side," he said, his words tight as he tried to suck in his sizeable beer belly. "Go on," he gasped. "Shoot."

Viv snapped a few pictures before pausing to check the shots on her digital screen.

"Where do you want me next?" Eldin asked after gasping for several deep breaths. "Over by the fire-place? I could build a fire. I know how."

"That's good to know. And I would take you up on it in a heartbeat…" Viv checked her flash. "…if it wasn't ninety plus degrees outside."

"Forget the fire. I'll just hold a few chunks of wood. Maybe I should take my shirt off to look like I've been out chopping all day—"

"No," she cut in, desperate to ignore the sudden image of Eldin shirtless. "These are supposed to be action shots. A day in the life of stuff." She stared deep into his eyes to press her point home. "That means natural."

He looked confused for a split-second before he seemed to relax. "Let me just straighten the magazines here like I do every night on account of my granny and her dad-burned group are always messing things up. Why, it takes days to get this lobby back to normal after one of her danged meetings."

"Shame on you for talking about an old lady," said a crackling voice as an ancient-looking woman walked from the back room.

She wore a purple flower-print dress, white orthopedic shoes and knee-high panty hose. She had a shock of white hair curled into tight sausages that covered her head like a football helmet. Bifocals hung from a chain around her neck and sat low on her nose.

"If I was a few years younger," she continued as she deposited a cardboard box on the counter and wagged a finger at Eldin, "I'd take a skillet to your hind end. Just pay him no nevermind," she turned to Viv. "He hates my meetings because he has to give up the TV and bide his time until we're finished."

"You took three hours last time," Eldin whined. "I missed *Grey's Anatomy* and *So You Think You Can Dance.*"

"You watch too much TV. You ought to be doing other things with your time."

"Like what?"

"The front walkway needs power washing."

"But that'll take hours."

"That's the idea."

"But I been standing all day. My feet hurt."

"That's 'cause you're putting on too much weight." She snatched the Snickers bar out of his pocket. "Steer clear of the snack machine, and you won't have such a big gut puttin' so much pressure on your tootsies. Why, I been standing over eighty years, and my feet don't hurt a bit."

"But that's my dessert." Eldin eyed the candy bar in her hand. "Dessert is one of the four basic food groups."

"Is not."

"Is too. There's fruit, potatoes, steak and dessert. A man needs all of 'em if he wants to keep up his stamina."

The old woman seemed to soften as she eyed him. "I s'pose you'll need your energy to handle that power washer." She handed the candy bar back to him. "Take it and skedaddle." She waved a hand and motioned him out. "My students will be here in less than fifteen minutes. I'm Winona Atkins," she added, turning to Viv. "Are you the one who called yesterday about joining my group?"

"I'm afraid not. I'm a guest. Room 12."

"You're the one from California? The one with the flashy sports car?"

"Guilty."

She seemed to think. "Had me a little Pinto once. It wasn't much too look at, but my husband—rest his soul—souped up the engine for me. It was the fastest ride in town. Faster than that old Mustang Merle Shanks used to hot rod around in, I'll tell you that much." She opened the edges of the cardboard box. One shriveled hand dove into the box, and she pulled out an enormous purple vibrator—

Oh, no, she didn't.

Viv blinked, but sure enough it was purple, it was a vibrator and it was enormous. A neon blue version followed. Then an orange. A yellow. Pink. Aqua.

"What exactly does your group do?" Viv asked as she watched the old woman unpack the box as nonchalantly as if she were setting out crochet needles instead of sex toys.

"A little of this. A little of that." Winona shrugged. "Tonight we're learning how to give a blowjob without biting. We're also going to talk about how to respond when your partner approaches you about a blow job, or vice versa. You'd be surprised how many gals just ain't that good when it comes to tellin' their men what they want."

Tell me about it.

"So it's like a self help class to overcome shyness?"

"It's a class to pull the stick out of your ass."

Viv couldn't help but smile. While the old woman had plenty of snow on the roof, she was all fire and spunk inside.

"I teach women how to loosen up and relax," Winona continued, "so's that they can enrich their relationships with their fellas. It's all about using what you got to spice things up and keep your man screaming for more. I'm a carnal coach. Coach Winona." She pulled a penis-shaped name tag out of her pocket and pinned it to the front of her dress.

"We also have refreshments," she added. "Mary Lou's bringing her famous pigs-in-a-blanket and Jennie Sue's making a coffee cake. I'm even baking a few batches of pleasure bites to get everyone feeling frisky. They're small, round little tastes of heaven made primarily of the one thing no sexually repressed woman can resist."

Viv arched an eyebrow. "Chocolate?"

"Alcohol." Winona adjusted her glasses. "See, I've got a lot of introverts in my class, like poor, timid Ellen Jenkins—she's the local librarian. That woman won't even send her hamburger back when they load it with ketchup instead of mustard. She sure as shootin' can't work up the nerve to tell Oren—that's her husband— that he's just not satisfying her in the sack. So instead of calling him out, she joined my class. She figured if she got better at doin' it, then she could make up for what he lacked. I had my doubts about that. Oren wasn't the best-looking catfish in the pond, and so the girls never paid him no nevermind growing up. He's definitely a plate short of a place setting when it comes to physical relations. But Ellen paid her registration in full, and I wasn't one to argue with cold hard cash.

Anyhow, sober she could barely sit through a lecture without blushing. A few pleasure bites, and she all but fought me for the pole when I did my strip-your-way-into-his-heart seminar."

"They sound very effective."

"And pretty darned tasty. You really ought to sit in tonight and try a few for yourself. You might even pick up some pointers on how to be more sexy." She wiggled her eyebrows. "I'm going to reveal my ten Do-Me-Baby Commandments after we finish blow jobs. It's a special list I put together over the past few months based on my own experience as a vibrant, sexually active woman." When Viv looked doubtful, she added, "Back in the day, that is. I'm not nearly as sexually active as I should be right now on account of I'm still pining for my late husband."

That and she was still waiting on Morty Donovan to haul his carcass out of his rocking chair and ask her for a date. Morty was in charge of Bingo over at the senior center. He also had the whitest dentures in town because his grandson was a cosmetic dentist, and Morty got free bleaching with every visit.

"If you can manage to learn all ten of them," Winona said, "there ain't a man alive who'll be able to resist you."

While Viv had no trouble consuming liquids, anything solid (even if it was one hundred and eighty proof) was completely off-limits. Even more, the last thing she needed was a how-to list to beef up her sex appeal. She'd been oozing vampire mojo for over two centuries. She already knew that no man could resist her.

But Garret Sawyer wasn't a man.

He was a vampire.

Larger than life. Tall, dark and totally immune to her supernatural charms because he had plenty of his own.

Forget being a persuasive, seductive female vampire. From here on out, it was all about being a persuasive, seductive female, period.

A scary thought for a woman who'd been turned before she'd even lost her virginity. A woman who'd been so desperate for survival that she'd never learned how to rely on good, old-fashioned feminine wiles.

No flirting or teasing. No licking her lips and batting her eyelashes. No being overly affectionate one minute and hard-to-get the next.

She'd never played games with men.

She'd never had to.

"The first class is free. What do you say?" Winona asked, arching one silver eyebrow. "You want to join us?"

Viv grabbed a rubber penis and glanced around. "Just tell me where to sit."

5

THE HALLWAY BENEATH the house was pitch-black, but it didn't matter. Garret's gaze sliced through the darkness and fixated on the door knob. Yes, he could see it, all right. He just couldn't get his fingers around it because it kept moving.

A little to the left…

A little to the right…

There.

Wood creaked, and the door slammed inward.

A single lamp burned on the nightstand and pushed back the shadows. The walls of the massive room seemed to vibrate. The plasma TV mounted on the opposite wall swam in front of him.

He meant to pick his leg up and take a step inside, but damned if his body would cooperate. He slid forward. The rug caught the tip of his boot, and he tripped. His shoulder hit the edge of a thick maple dresser. His head slammed into the mirror. Glass shattered and pain cracked open his skull. He doubled over. His stomach churned and his throat burned and—

Shit.

He shouldn't have drank so friggin' much.

No matter how desperate he was to forget.

Images of Viv pushed into his head, and he could see her looming above him. Her long, silky black hair falling down around her shoulders. Her deep blue eyes glittering with pleasure. Moonlight bathed her pale breasts, her nipples red and ripe and so damned tempting. She braced her hands against his chest as she straddled him. Her head fell back, and her eyes closed. She started to move, her body lifting and sliding as her heat slithered down over his cock, and she rode him hard and deep and—

Shit. Shit. Shit.

Garret forced his eyes open and stared through a watery haze. A few blinks, and his vivid memories faded into the polished wood paneling. He gripped the edge of the dresser and hauled himself to his feet. Three steps, and his knee caught the nightstand. Wood crashed. Shafts of light bounced off the walls as the lamp toppled over and rolled across the hardwood floor.

The noise knifed at his throbbing temples. He fell to his knees, floundering for the king-sized bed. Finally his hands made contact with the down comforter, and relief rushed through him. He needed to lie down for a little while.

Sleep.

When he woke up he would realize that it was all just a dream. Viv wasn't really here in town, and he didn't still want her so badly he could hardly stand it.

He sprawled on the bed and closed his eyes, determined to shut out the thundering in his head, the pain in his body and her.

Especially her.

But he hadn't drank nearly enough for that, and so the damnable vision followed him into the blackness. Teasing and taunting and reminding him of just how good they'd been together.

How good they could be again if Garret let his guard down.

But he wouldn't.

He'd been burned once before, and he wasn't jumping into the fire again.

No matter how much he suddenly wanted to.

HE FELT LIKE horse shit.

A big, thick pile of the stuff that had been baked a day or two in the hot, sweltering Texas sun.

Garret pushed to a sitting position, his muscles screaming with the effort. He blinked against the fluorescent bulb hanging overhead and willed his eyes to focus.

They watered instead, and he blinked. Once. Twice. He raked a hand over his face and glanced at his watch. It was just a little after six in the evening. The sun wouldn't set for at least another hour, which explained his exhaustion.

And his pounding head? He had to give the empty whiskey bottle next to him all the credit for that one.

He fell back to the mattress and closed his eyes.

A hangover.

He had a friggin' hangover.

Not that the concept was foreign to vampires. Just the opposite, in fact. A vampire had heightened senses, which meant that everything—taste, touch, smell, sight, sound—was magnified a thousand times over. If the average human could tie one on with a few beers, a vampire could get rip-roaring drunk on a helluva lot less. He could also pass out quicker from the effects and hurt even more the morning after.

Or, in his case, the night after.

He'd learned that the hard way the night Viv had left him. He'd been so drunk that he'd wandered out into the woods and passed out. The first rays of sunlight were just creeping over the horizon when he'd finally come to, and he'd suffered some serious burns before he'd managed to get his ass up and out of there.

He hadn't exceeded his two drink limit since.

He pushed his eyelids open again and swept a gaze around the shambles that had once been his bedroom. His dresser lay on its side, clothes spilled out onto the hardwood floor. His nightstand was upended. A lamp lay several feet away near a big screen TV. The bedroom door sat wide open, the rug bunched where he'd stumbled in last night.

He glanced up at the open beams of the ceiling. He'd left the rafters exposed when he'd bought the ranch house and converted the basement into a "safe" space— the perfect place for a vampire to sleep while the rest of the world went about their daily business. He'd wanted the rooms to seem larger and less cramped.

He hated being cooped up. Smothered. Cursed.

He stared at the door situated directly across the hall. The basement consisted of two rooms separated by a main hallway that led upstairs to the kitchen.

Newly made vampire, Dillon Cash, had been living in the opposite room while Garret had helped him learn the ropes of being undead. Meanwhile, Meg Sweeney, Dillon's best friend and now his girlfriend, had been helping him learn the ins and outs of great sex.

The great sex had quickly morphed into a bona fide relationship. Dillon and Meg were now living together at her place, and Garret was once again on his own in the sprawling ranch house with its state-of-the-art security system.

Garret's spread sat on over one hundred and twenty acres. The two-story rock house, as well as the barn and bunk station, had surveillance cameras around the entire perimeter.

But while the cameras could warn him of intruders, they couldn't do anything when it came to sunlight, and so he made sure to stay below ground until the sun set.

He smiled. Most of the old myths people believed about vampires didn't hold true. They didn't turn into bats or sleep in coffins. They weren't the least bit bothered by crucifixes or holy water. But sunlight... Talk about frying to a crisp.

A thought struck, and panic bolted through him.

He threw his legs over the side of the bed and pushed to his feet. The floor tilted for a long second before finally settling down. He picked his way through the bedroom and out into the hallway. He stumbled up the basement steps and sure enough, the door at the top stood wide open.

Because he'd been too shit-faced to remember to close it.

A shaft of light spilled down into the corridor and brought him to an abrupt halt.

He stared at the sliver of fading daylight and couldn't help but remember the long days in the saddle when he'd been just a man.

Before he'd gone off to fight for Texas independence, he'd helped on his family's horse farm. He'd set a horse for hours on end back then, rounding up wild broncs and breaking them. He could still see the stretch of empty plain in front of him, feel the sun beating down on the top of his head, the warmth surrounding him.

Before he could stop himself, he reached out. His fingertips brushed the light and pain wrenched through him. A sharp hiss vibrated his vocal chords.

The smell of burned flesh filled his nostrils as he stared down at his seared fingertips. A wave of regret washed through him.

Regret for the warmth he'd lost.

The life.

The love.

He forced the last notion aside. He hadn't loved Viv. He hadn't, and so there was no use regretting what he'd never had. As for his life... He missed it, all right. He missed the sun and his mama's homemade cornbread and freedom.

He retraced his steps back down into the basement and spent the next half hour cleaning up the mess he'd made. By the time he'd finished and taken a shower, dusk had settled around the house.

Only shadows crowded the staircase as he made his way upstairs and into the kitchen.

Unlike the rest of the ancient ranch house with its stone fireplace and authentic hardwood floors, the kitchen had been completely redone. Black granite countertops ran along the perimeter. There were new appliances and hand-carved oak cabinets. It was a chef's dream and a constant reminder of the man he'd once been.

The man he wanted to be again.

Grasping the stainless-steel handle of the refrigerator, he hauled open the door and retrieved a plastic bag of blood from one of the shelves. He nuked the bag to warm it up and cut the coldness, and then poured himself a glass. The first drop hit his tongue and sent a shiver through him. Warmth slid down his throat and spiraled in his gut, but it didn't ease the clenching inside of him.

If anything, it made it worse.

While the bagged stuff provided sustenance, it didn't give him the same satisfaction as sinking his fangs into a sweet, warm neck. Feeling the pulse against his tongue. Tasting the life that pumped through someone else's veins.

It was pure ecstasy, and at the same time, the worst kind of pain because it only made him want more.

That's why he refrained from biting as much as possible. Because it increased the craving as much as it satisfied it.

His hands trembled as he poured another glass and pulled out his cell.

"You sound like shit," Jake McCann said when Garret asked if he was at the shop yet.

Jake was his best friend and business partner. He was also a vampire, thanks to Garret.

It had been the anniversary of Garret's turning and he'd instinctively returned to the place of his death to relive those last few moments when his humanity had slipped away and the hunger—the damnable hunger— had seized control. Like any other vampire experiencing the turning, he'd been out of control. Jake had crossed his path, and Garret had attacked him. And then he'd tried to right his wrong by giving Jake back the life that had been stolen from him.

Or rather, a new life.

One born and bred in darkness.

He'd doomed Jake to the same fate, just as Jake had doomed Dillon. Jake hadn't been the one to attack the young man. No, Garret had done that during the most recent anniversary of his turning. In yet another thirsty craze, he'd attacked Dillon and inadvertently left him on Death's doorstep. Luckily, Jake had been on hand to turn Dillon before he completely bled out.

"What the hell happened to you?" Jake asked.

"Two bottles of Jack."

"Only two?"

"I lost count after two." Before Jake could push for more information, Garret rushed on, "Did you finish the design on the Harwell bike?" Ethan Harwell was CEO of a multi-million dollar oil company who'd commissioned a specialty chopper that incorporated his company's theme and logo.

"I'm putting the final specs on the oil well shaped spokes tonight. Late tonight. It's Saturday night."

"And?"

"Saturday night is date night. I promised Nikki I would take her out." Nikki was Jake's girlfriend and the best hairdresser in town. She was also human, and Jake meant for her to stay that way. He refused to turn her. Not while there was still hope of reclaiming his own humanity.

Hope that hinged on Garret.

Since he had sired Jake and Jake had sired Dillon, finding and destroying the vamp who'd sired Garret would start a domino effect that would free all three of them.

"We're meeting Meg and Dillon over in Karnes County for the rodeo. After the bull riding, we'll head back to the shop and catch up."

"Since when do you like bull riding?"

"Since forever." Jake had been a real cowboy back in the day. He could ride and rope almost as well as Garret. "Why don't you come with us?" Jake added.

"I've got a meeting with someone about some free PR for the shop."

"You work too much, bro."

"Yeah, well, somebody has to while the rest of you are goofing off."

"It's called having fun. You should try it sometime."

"Trust me. I have plenty of fun."

"You mean plenty of one-night stands."

"Same thing." At least, it had been. A long, long time ago when he'd first turned.

But after one hundred and eighty years and too many women to count, he didn't enjoy it nearly as much as he used to. He wanted more than sex. He wanted an actual relationship. He wanted someone to love. Someone to love him.

"He needs a real date," came Nikki's voice in the background.

"I don't need a date."

"I don't know, buddy." Since settling down with Nikki, Jake had done a complete one-eighty when it came to women and relationships. Ditto for Dillon since he'd landed Meg. While Garret knew that a real relationship could exist between a vampire and a woman, he knew his buddies were the exception rather than the rule. Dillon and Jake had gotten lucky, and Garret had never been long on luck.

"A date might lighten you up," Jake continued. "Take the edge off. You sound really tense."

"I'm fine."

"Nikki's got this friend—"

"Later." Garret hit the Off button. He was over one hundred and eighty years old, for Christ's sake. He didn't date.

Dating implied liking and liking implied a relationship, and a relationship implied a mutual give and take between two individuals. Other than fantastic sex, Garret had nothing to offer a woman.

Not until he managed to find and destroy the vampire who'd made him.

He chugged the rest of his blood, grabbed his Stetson and headed outside to the barn.

For so long he'd run from the past, from the man he'd been. He'd dressed differently—all bad-ass biker with his leather and bandanas and chains. He'd avoided small towns and clung to the cities, desperate to trade the rolling pastureland for miles and miles of concrete. He'd even refused to sit a horse.

But seeing Jake so determined to break the curse, to have a real future with his human girlfriend, Nikki Braxton, had reminded Garret of the man he'd been.

A man who'd loved horses and lived in the saddle, one who'd enjoyed the fresh air and freedom. A man who'd fought hard for what he believed in—his family and his land and his right to have both.

Until he'd been turned.

Even then, he'd held tight to the man he'd been. He'd wanted to save himself. He'd fought the damnable hunger for so long, and he'd kept fighting. But eventually, he'd gotten tired. Exhausted. Giving in had been easier.

No more.

He was through running. Forgetting.

He still hadn't climbed back into the saddle yet, but that was just a matter of time. He'd recently purchased several horses, and taming them would take a while.

One in particular—Delilah. She was the toughest of the bunch and the most stubborn.

So was Garret.

He wouldn't give up on her any more than he would give up on finding the vampire who'd turned him.

He held tight to the thought and spent a half hour pitching hay and pouring oats.

When he finished, he checked the gates, grabbed his chopper keys and headed into town to find out what Viviana Darland really wanted from him.

6

IT WAS TOO SMALL, too cramped, too quiet.

Viv wanted to move, to open the door and crawl out of the stifling closet. The sun had already set, and there was safety in the darkness. Right?

She touched the sticky wetness soaking her chest. The blood wasn't coming as fast as when Molly had first staked her, but it was still flowing, saturating her shirt and oozing onto the scarred wooden floor of the abandoned cabin.

She tried for a breath of air and a white-hot pain cut through her. Molly had been aiming for her heart, but she'd missed. Barely.

Still, the puncture hurt like a sonofabitch, and she was still bleeding heavily.

With every beat of her heart, more blood gushed from the open wound and made her wonder if—despite the fact that they'd missed her heart—she might die anyway.

Maybe this was it.

Her last few moments in existence.

The past flashed through her mind as she lay there,

like images advertising the birth of America on the History channel. The names echoed in her head.

Names she would never forget.

She saw Jimmy, the dying confederate soldier she'd gathered in her arms when she'd found him sprawled on the battlefield. She heard the anguish in his voice as he begged her to save him. She felt the tightening in her chest as she tried to resist.

But he kept begging, and her own heart kept hurting, until she gave in. She leaned over, sank her fangs into his neck and tasted the sweet heat. Pure ecstasy rolled through her body, along with a rush of dizzying energy, followed by a wave of regret.

Because as much as she wanted to save him, she knew the hunger he'd soon experience would be far worse than death.

She knew, but she turned him anyway because she couldn't help herself. She couldn't watch him die. She couldn't watch anyone die.

Never again.

Fast forward to an Apache raid. Or what was left of one.

She saw herself wandering through the demolished camp. The voices of the dying echoed in her ears. One man in particular called out to her. Travis. He was a farmer whose wife and three children had just been abducted. He was their only hope. He had to follow them. Save them.

But first he had to stop bleeding.

"Please," he begged and she couldn't resist. Not the desperation in his voice or the sweet scent curling in the air, luring her closer to his slaughtered body.

Her nostrils flared, her hunger roared, and she dipped her head. She lapped at the blood pulsing from one particular wound and awareness ripped through her. Her senses came alive, and it was as if an amplifier switched on in her head.

The whisper of the wind became a roar as it whipped through the trees. Crickets buzzed so loudly that she wanted to cover her ears. Horse hoofs thundered, and she flinched. Women pleaded and begged. Children whimpered and sniffled.

"Daddy!"

The desperate cry filled her head. A girl. Travis's youngest.

The hungry red haze that clouded her vision faded until his broken and battered face came into sharp focus. She saw the faint laugh lines around his eyes, the tiny scar that ran along his cheekbone, the deep pores of his skin. Recognition sparked as he stared up at her, and his lips moved.

"Do it," he rasped. "Help me. You have to."

She didn't. She shouldn't. She knew that.

At the same time, she couldn't stand the blood on her hands. The death on her conscience.

Not just Travis's death, but that of his wife and three daughters.

The horse hoofs kept pounding the ground, fading ever so slightly with each passing second. The little girl's voice faded, too. The crying. The pleading. The praying.

Anxiety rushed through Viv and she bared her fangs. Sinking them deep into her own wrist, she drew blood and held it to Travis's lips, and then she gave him back the precious life that was fast spilling out all over the dusty ground.

Her past kept replaying and she saw the others. Mary. James. Walter. Francis. Ruby. Ben. Molly and Cruz. Caroline. Mitchell. Richard. Loretta.

She could see their faces, hear their anguished voices, feel their pain and suffering.

She meant to say no to each and every one of them. To satisfy her own hunger and walk away. That's all that should have mattered. Feeding the beast inside of her.

At the same time, she couldn't resist the tears, the fear, the desperation. And so she tried to help, to cheat death out of yet another precious life.

But while she robbed death of victory, she didn't really save anyone. Rather, she doomed them to the hunger.

She'd doomed Garret.

Her stomach convulsed and her chest hurt and the blood kept coming, flooding the floor of the small closet. The ripe, sticky scent mingled with the smell of mothballs burned her nostrils. She held her hand to the wound and prayed for sleep. For peace.

She needed to heal. To forget.

Instead, she remembered.

Garret sprawled on the ground.

Broken.

Bleeding.

Dying.

"No!" She touched her lips to his and felt the weakness of his breath, the coldness of his skin.

One sharp slice to her neck, and her lifeblood spilled out, running in tiny rivulets down her skin, falling onto his pale lips, giving him new life all the while his old slipped away.

Slowly the color returned to his face, and his heartbeat grew strong and sure against the palm of her hand. She started to move, to leave him to heal before he opened his eyes and realized what had happened. She drew her hand away, but strong fingers clamped around hers and jerked her back down. A growl vibrated up his throat and his fangs flashed. He opened his eyes and instead of a warm chocolate, they burned a fierce, vivid violet. Her own heart catapulted with excitement, and lust rushed through her.

He turned her, pinning her to the ground.

She arched against him as he ripped her clothes away, until she felt his bare skin against her own. His hands swept up and down, touching her everywhere as he drew one nipple into his mouth and suckled her so hard that she moaned long and deep and… Ahhhhhh.

Strong, purposeful fingers found the wet heat between her legs and plunged inside. She gasped, wiggling her hips and drawing him another inch deeper… There. And there. And there.

Sensation coiled, and she felt herself winding tighter. Her hands roved over him, and she felt the bunch of his muscles as his excitement multiplied.

Her own hunger stirred, eager for a taste of the climax building inside of him. She threw her head back and arched her body, ready to feel his fangs sinking deep, and his hard erection pumping between her legs.

Sex and blood.

It was an intoxicating duo. One she'd never enjoyed with any man. Not at the same time.

But Garret was different.

Because she loved him.

Because he loved her.

Her body throbbed, and her hands trailed up and down his back, begging and pleading with him to touch her faster, harder, deeper—

The thought shattered as pain sliced through her from her collarbone, clear to her belly button. Her eyes went wide and she saw him poised above her, his hands wrapped around the sharp stake that protruded from her chest.

Blood spurted and steamed, the sound sizzling in her ears.

She opened her mouth, but her throat closed in on itself, and only a gurgle bubbled past her lips. Her gaze collided with his, and she saw the anger that burned a hot, vicious red in his eyes.

He knew the truth now, and he hated her for it.

"You did this to me," he growled. "You."

VIVIANA BOLTED UPRIGHT, her heart pounding.

She touched her chest, feeling only the soft cotton of her T-shirt and the warm metal of her St. Benedict medal.

No stake. No blood.

A dream.

That's all it had been.

Just a wild, horrific nightmare.

She and Garret hadn't made love that night, and he certainly hadn't tried to kill her.

He'd been too busy hurting. Dying.

She forced aside the memory of his body riddled with stab wounds and glanced toward the window. Shadows pushed past the edge of the blinds, a tell-tale sign that the sun had already set.

She eased from the bed and headed for the bathroom. She didn't bother to turn on the overhead bulb. She didn't need to. She could see every detail of the ancient powder-blue tile, the old-fashioned sink, the small medicine cabinet. She stared at her reflection in the mirror and noted the frantic rise and fall of her chest.

She was so freaked out she was actually breathing.

Closing her eyes, she counted to ten. Until the breaths stopped coming and her hands stopped trembling.

While the dream was a far cry from reality—she hadn't so much as kissed him that night—she had found him broken and bleeding, and she'd done her best to ease his pain.

She closed her eyes against a rush of tears and swallowed against the sudden tightening in her throat. She hadn't meant to hurt him.

But she had no doubt he would see things much differently.

That's why she'd left him so long ago. She'd been afraid to see the hatred in his eyes should he discover the truth.

She was still afraid.

He won't find out.

Even if he did, it wouldn't matter.

Cruz and Molly would catch her, and she wouldn't fight them. The curse would end and Garret would have his humanity back.

When they caught up with her.

She left the bathroom to double check the lock on the front door. As her hand closed over the doorknob, a strange niggling awareness worked its way up and down her spine. It was the same sensation she'd had up in Washington. When she'd been sensationalizing the Butcher's latest handiwork and Sheriff Keller had escorted her from the crime scene.

She could still feel his strong fingertips on her arm, hear the leaves crunching beneath his boots as they'd walked down the mountain, smell the sharp scent of pine trees and fresh blood and something else…

Someone.

They were getting closer. She knew it. She felt it. But while the feeling was there, it wasn't nearly as strong as it had been in Washington.

She double-checked the lock and headed back to the bathroom. Drawing back the shower curtain, she turned the shower on full force and stepped beneath the icy spray.

Dunking her head under the sluice of water, she closed her eyes and fought to control the frantic beating of her heart. Eventually, the tears faded. The fear started to seep away and spiral down the drain along with the ice-cold water.

By the time she stepped from the shower and reached for a fluffy towel, she'd managed to tamp down on her regret and gather her control.

Think tonight.

Think seduction.

Think Winona's ten Do-Me-Baby commandments.

Or, at least most of them.

While she fully intended to bat her eyes and lick her lips as often as possible, she wasn't so sure she was going to slap Garret's ass or tickle his balls (numbers seven and eight on the list). At least not until they were already naked and in bed.

That was the goal.

To turn him on to the point that he toppled her onto the nearest horizontal surface and initiated the sex so she didn't have to.

She'd spent an eternity being the aggressor, mesmerizing men and bending them to her will, acting rather than reacting.

No more.

Yes, she would be suggestive, seductive, inviting. But she wouldn't make the first move. She was leaving that up to Garret.

She had to.

That's why he'd been the first and only man to give her an orgasm. He'd been the aggressor. He'd been the one to take the initiative and approach her first—before she'd "vamped" him. He'd swept her off her feet and ravished her, and all because of his own passionate nature. Because he'd really and truly wanted her of his own free will. Unlike the others, who'd been puppets manipulated by her vamp charm.

She wanted Garret to want her again. She wanted to taste his excitement, his fervor, his passion once more because she knew it would feed her own and give her one last climax.

The thing was, she hadn't been trying to attract him back then. It had just happened. One look and bam, he'd been over the top for her. Out of control.

But now… She would have to use everything in her mortal female power (as untried as it was) to tempt him past the point of no return.

With that thought in mind, she stashed her St. Benedict medal in her suitcase and pulled out her clothes.

She didn't have a tank top and Daisy Duke shorts (commandment number two), so she opted for the closest thing she could find—a red silk shell and a fitted black skirt. She bypassed the undies (commandment number one), added a spritz of perfume to the inside of each thigh and her belly button (number four) and donned her outfit.

She finished with a pair of stilettos and grabbed her camera bag. She had the rest of her supplies—backdrops, lighting, extra cameras, several stands—already packed in her car. Taking one final look at the list of notes she'd taken during Winona's class, she mentally checked off the first five commandments (the rest would have to wait until she came face-to-face with Garret) and fought down a wave of nerves.

By the time the evening ended, he would be begging her for sex.

Or so she desperately hoped.

7

GARRET WASN'T begging Viv for sex.

He wasn't begging her for anything—because he wasn't there.

Disappointment rushed through her, along with a burst of anxiety as she walked into the spacious machine shop that housed Skull Creek Choppers.

It was just after sunset. Shadows crowded outside the glass windows that lined the front wall facing Main Street. Fluorescent lights blazed overhead, illuminating the stainless steel work tables covered with tools. Some she recognized—screwdrivers and wrenches and pliers—but most were totally foreign to her. An assortment of saw blades covered one twelve foot surface. An industrial strength welding unit overflowed a nearby corner. A grinder and several sprayers edged the sidelines while three large work tables dominated the center of the room. On top of one sat the shiny silver skeleton of a motorcycle. On another sat a large chunk of metal that vaguely resembled a gas tank. The third table held several long strips of metal that had been cut to resemble lightning bolts. They sat next to something that looked like a large welder. It had clamps and a curved wheel.

While Viv was no expert, she would have been willing to bet the machine had something to do with shaping and molding the fenders.

Her ears perked. She tuned in to the whir of the air conditioner, the tick-tock of a nearby clock, the hum of the massive computer system that sat in a small adjacent office just to the right. Another wall of windows separated the space from the actual shop.

There was nothing else. No deep, familiar rumble of his voice or the pounding of his heart or the pulse of his blood.

Her nose twitched, and she caught a sharp whiff of oil and engine fluid. The musky mingling of rubber and exhaust. The sterile scent of industrial strength soap and disinfectant.

The place was empty, all right. Despite the lights that blazed and the door that had been left unlocked.

Then again, this was a small town with zero crime.

She knew the type, which was why she'd made it her business to stick to the big cities. For the anonymity. The throng of people. The safety.

Garret was asking for trouble settling in such a rinky-dink place.

That, or he was just tired of running. Maybe he wanted to settle down and have the normalcy she'd robbed him of so long ago.

Guilt niggled at her the way it always did when she thought of the past, but she pushed it aside this time.

She was through living with the regret. She was doing something about it now. She was giving back.

But first…

She cast another glance around and blew out an exasperated breath. She busied herself snapping a few pictures, desperate to calm her trembling hands and rein in the sexual frustration that whipped through her.

He would be back soon, and she would get on with the matter at hand—seducing him past the point of no return.

She was armed and ready. She'd dabbed a few drops of Winona's Strawberry Seduction behind each ear. She'd gone over her notes another ten times before climbing out of the car. She was in full-blown seduction mode, her body quivering in anticipation, and he was MIA.

For now.

He would be back soon. He'd agreed to the date, and he'd always kept his word. He'd probably gone out for supplies or coffee or a quick bite.

The last thought stirred a rush of jealousy that made her stiffen.

She shifted her attention to the bike, eager to ignore the sudden image that popped into her head. Garret leaning over some woman, holding her, sinking his fangs deep—

She shook away the vision and reached out to trace the silver metallic skull and cross bones etched into the chopper's rear fender. A flaming silver skull blazed on the gas tank. The seat was rounded and curved with skulls embossed on the leather. The rims were made up of a center skull with four metal-shaped "bones" for spokes. Every detail, from the skull-shaped headlight to the red cross-bone brake lights played into the theme. It was the coolest and most unusual bike she'd ever seen.

Even more, it was sexy.

It was Garret.

A tiny thrill ripped through her. Sure, it was just a pile of metal—a motorcycle, not a man—but the man had been the one to put it together.

He'd smoothed and molded the steel. He'd attached the pieces. He'd touched and shaped and put his heart and soul into the machine to the point that she couldn't see it and not think about him.

It looked like him—sleek and masculine and dangerous. It felt like him—hard and cool and stirring. It even smelled like him—a heady mixture of rich leather and fresh air and pure adrenaline that made her heart beat that much faster.

Before she could stop herself, she set her camera on a nearby table and hiked her skirt up. Leather met her bare bottom as she straddled the seat and awareness crackled through her. Goosebumps danced up and down her skin and her nipples pebbled.

She wiggled for a better position and sensation speared her. She gasped and caught her lip against a sharp, sweet zap of lust.

No, no, no!

The chant echoed through her head because this was

not what she wanted. She'd had a zillion orgasms before, but none with a man.

Just him.

Only him.

At the same time, it felt so good, and she was so wound up. A little rocking back and forth, some wiggling side to side, and she could relieve some of the tension winding her so tight. No way would she make it through the first five minutes without doing something totally crazy. Like jump his bones the moment he walked in the door.

A disastrous move, she knew.

While he still wanted her—she'd seen it in his eyes— he didn't want to want her. To feel the attraction. The lust.

He was still hurt. Angry. Furious.

No way would he let his guard down, stop resisting what he felt for her and simply act on it.

Not yet.

She had to get him to relax, which meant she needed to bide her time and seduce him slowly.

Right.

She was too wound up. Too close to pinning him against the nearest wall and ravishing his hot, hunky body. She needed to take the edge off.

Right here.

Right now.

She leaned forward to grasp the handlebars. Her bottom slid a scant inch across the cool seat. Leather rasped her clit and desire knifed through her. She shivered. Her vision blurred. Her ears rang. Pleasure gripped her for a long, delicious moment and she caught her bottom lip.

And then she adjusted her grip, braced her thighs and started to ride.

SHE WANTED SEX.

The realization echoed in Garret's head as he stood in the office of Skull Creek Choppers and stared through the glass wall that overlooked the machine shop.

A realization that had nothing to do with the fact that he was a highly sensitive, mind-reading vampire and everything to do with the fact that he was a full-blooded male.

His heart jumped, pounding harder and faster. His muscles went tight, his spine stiff. His gut clenched and his cock throbbed as his gaze roved over the woman perched atop his latest custom chopper.

It was a project he was doing for a high profile rock star. The lead singer for some insanely popular band. Jake hadn't wanted to do the bike because they were already so busy and the guy wanted it ASAP, but Garret hadn't been able to pass up a PR op. The exposure alone would be worth the added stress of getting the bike done on time.

Even so, Garret had tacked on a hefty fee for a quick turn-around. They would make three times their usual amount on this one project. With Jake swamped, Garret had done both the design and the build. He'd put on the final touches—a silver skull gas cap and a cross-bones kick stand—just yesterday.

The finished product had been, hands-down, the most beautiful sight he'd ever seen.

Until now.

He watched as Viv arched her body. Her head fell back. Her long, dark hair spilled down her shoulders. Her eyes were closed, her neck arched. Her full, pink lips parted on a gasp as she slid her bare ass across his leather seat…

Beautiful.

The notion stuck as he watched her move. Her breasts quivered. Her nipples pressed provocatively against the thin material of her blouse. She slid along the seat again and her hands tightened on the handlebars, her knuckles going white. A pink flush crept up her neck, over the frantic throb of her pulse and higher into her face. She worked the skirt up an inch higher so she could spread her legs wider and make better contact.

His mouth went dry, and his heart shifted into overdrive. A sliver of excitement worked its way through him, followed by a rush of whoa, buddy.

She wanted sex, all right.

What vampire didn't?

It was the nature of the beast.

The consequence of the curse.

And it was the only explanation for his nearly irresistible urge to stride into the room, haul her off the bike, shove her up against the nearest wall and plunge deep, deep inside of her hot, tight body.

Where he'd been a slave to her hunger before, he was now a slave to his own.

He sure as hell didn't want her because he actually felt something for her.

Or rather, because he thought he felt something.

He'd thought a lot of things way back when. He'd thought that maybe they would get married. Settle down. Raise horses and a family. That they would spend Christmases decorating a tree and hanging up stockings. That he would work the farm while she kept house, and at night they would fall into bed together.

But nothing had been real.

Not her.

Not his feelings for her.

Not his damnable dreams.

It had all been an illusion spawned by her vamp powers because she wanted sex from him. Energy. Strength.

He knew, because he'd created the same illusion for the women he'd fed off of over the years. He'd mesmerized them with his charm. Swept them off their feet with his hot, wet kisses. Spoiled them for any other man with his sexual expertise. And then he'd taken from them.

He'd done to other women exactly what she'd done to him. With one exception. He hadn't talked of dreams and the future and a real, bona fide relationship. He'd wanted one thing and one thing only—a one-night stand—and he'd made his needs crystal clear. He hadn't toyed with anyone's emotions.

It had all been about sex.

The hunger roared to life, as demanding as ever. His groin tightened and his body trembled and he barely managed to resist the need screaming inside of him. His fingers balled and his muscles bunched as he turned and walked back outside.

He had to get a grip.

Resist.

The shadows welcomed him as he moved silently around the side of the building toward the back parking lot. A few feet shy, he stopped and leaned against the cold steel.

The amp in his head switched on, bombarding him with sounds. The chirp of crickets. The squeal of tires as someone burned rubber down the street. The tick-tick of a parking meter a block away.

Her soft moans pushed through the blare of noise, and he knew she was close to coming. So damned close…

He drew several deep breaths, hoping to cool the fire that raged inside of him.

Fat chance.

He closed his eyes, counted to ten, and did his best to concentrate on the sound of his own voice rather than her whisper-soft oohs and ahhs.

He hit ten and kept on going.

It wasn't until he murmured one hundred that he finally managed to soothe his frantic heartbeat and regain his composure.

When he could think of something other than the

sexy woman riding his newest creation just a few feet away, he headed back around to the front of the shop.

At one time, the place had been a service station. The ancient pumps were still there, still working, along with the original Davey's Fill-r-Up ball that rotated atop an iron pole. He had a thing for vintage, and so he'd left the old Coke machine, along with a Fanta sign and one advertising Mmm-Mmm Good Moonpies. The only thing to clue anyone in that the place had been turned into a state-of-the-art chopper shop was the neon blue Home of Skull Creek Choppers that hummed in the front window and the hi-tech security pad that sat next to the entrance.

Punching in the code (the door locked automatically every time it shut), he walked inside and went out of his way to make as much noise as possible.

He slammed the door a little harder than usual and hit the edge of the filing cabinet. The metal rattled and shook, the sound bouncing off the office walls. He paused to shuffle papers and move a few things around near the computer.

He didn't have to look through the windows to see if she'd heard him. He heard her loud and clear.

Her surprised whimper, followed by the faint gasp of leather and the grumble of steel as she scrambled off the seat. The soft click as her shoes hit the concrete. The swish-swish of fabric as she shoved the skirt down to a modest level.

Disappointment rushed through him, feeding the insane urge to waltz in and rip the damned thing off of her. He wanted her naked and ready and—

Whoa. The word thundered through his head, yanking him from his ridiculous thoughts and reminding him that he couldn't. He wouldn't.

Not Viv.

Not ever again.

Bracing himself, he hauled open the door that separated them and walked into the shop.

8

FINALLY.

That was the first thought on Viv's mind when she heard the door open and close. Despite the fact that she'd almost been caught having a pretty fantastic orgasm.

Sex was a necessity. Like oxygen to the average human. She didn't usually feel guilty over it. Or mortified. Or embarrassed.

Not until she soothed her skirt down one final time, hooked a now damp tendril of hair behind one ear and turned toward Garret.

He wore a soft cotton T-shirt that molded to his broad shoulders and solid chest. Worn denim cupped his crotch and hugged his muscular legs. He wore the black Stetson she remembered from the bar. The hat brim tipped low, casting a shadow over the upper half of his face.

Her gaze collided with his and there was just something about the gleam in his pale blue eyes that said Gotcha.

Heat flooded her cheeks and awareness sizzled up and down her spine. "I, um, was just seeing how she handles," she blurted, suddenly desperate for a plausible excuse.

He tossed his keys on a nearby work table. His boots thudded on the stained concrete floor as he stepped toward her. "What's the verdict?"

"Nice." And how. "That is—" she licked her lips, "—the handlebars felt good. Solid."

He seemed almost angry at her answer. His gaze narrowed, and his jaw went tense. But then she licked her lips, and his attention snagged on the sweeping motion of her tongue. Just like that, his defenses seemed to lapse, and his body relaxed just a fraction. Strong, sensuous lips crooked in a faint smile. "So you had a pretty good grip, then?"

"Very."

The animosity between them slipped away, and the air charged with a sudden awareness that made her spine tingle. He was flirting with her. Teasing. Tempting.

Because he'd seen her.

His eyes sparkled like ice reflecting rays of sunlight and her tummy tingled. "How about the seat? How did that feel?"

Fan-friggin'-tastic.

That's what she wanted to say, but she caught her bottom lip just in case she was overreacting and he wasn't being nearly as forward as she hoped.

"Comfortable." Viv nodded. "Not too hard. Not too soft. Just—" she swallowed against her suddenly dry throat "—right."

"That's good to know." He raked a gaze over her,

from her head to her toes and back up again. His attention lingered on several key places.

Her nipples throbbed, and she felt the sudden wetness between her legs. Her heart pounded with excitement.

"You know," his voice slid into her ears and rumbled across her nerve endings, "if you really want to get a feel for her, you need to crank her up." He hooked a leg over and straddled the seat. Large, strong hands rested on the gas tank. "You don't want a bike that vibrates too much." His gaze caught and held hers. "You need a nice, steady hum so you can get into a groove when you're on the road."

He was flirting with her, all right.

His words stirred a very vivid picture of the two of them zooming along, finding their groove. Moonlight spilled down around them. Her hands gripped the handlebars while his hands stroked the wet flesh between her legs.

Despite her orgasm, she felt herself winding right back up. His scent filled her head, and the raw timbre of his voice tickled her ears. His tall, sexy body filled up her line of vision.

She shook her head, desperate to remember her objective.

Slow. Easy.

"I, um, wouldn't know. I've never actually ridden a motorcycle."

Liar. That's what his gaze seemed to say, but he didn't voice the sentiment out loud. Instead, he shrugged.

"That's a shame. You're really missing out. There's nothing like climbing on the back of one of these babies and cutting loose."

Amen.

She could still feel the handlebars in her grasp, the gas tank between her legs, the cool, delicious leather rasping her—

"—try it at least once if you're going to write about it."

His voice shattered the memory and snatched her back to the present. "Excuse me?"

"I said you'll have to take at least one ride." His gaze sparked. "A real ride," he added, "if you really want to get it right for your article." Suspicion worked its way into his expression. "That's why you're here, right? To get info for your article?"

"Of course." Not that he believed her. She could see the doubt in his guarded expression and the way his body stiffened. The muscles in his arms rippled and tensed. "Why else?" She went for the wide-eyed, innocent look that had rated number nine on Winona's list.

It was a look that appealed to a man's baser instincts. It said poor little old me needs big strong you, and it was guaranteed to make a man forget everything—the football game, the yard work, the cute little honey washing her car next door.

He stared at her, as if he could see the answer if he looked long and hard enough. He couldn't. Thankfully. And so he finally shrugged. "It just seems a little too coincidental that you showed up here. Now. Don't you think?"

"Not really. Stranger things happen all the time." Before he could say anything else, she rushed on, "You're right. I definitely need to take a real ride if I want to write about the activity with any enthusiasm. But since I'm out of my element I'd really like to get some background info first." What was she saying? If the man wanted to give her a ride, then all the better. But a ride and a ride were two different things, and if they got that close, she could forget slow and easy. She would take the lead and be the aggressor and that would surely kill her chances at an orgasm.

Better to slow down for now. A little small talk and his guard would ease. He would go back to flirting with her, and the situation would escalate from there. "I'd really like to snap a few pictures right now."

"If I didn't know better, I'd say you were scared. But then you're a vampire, and vampires aren't scared of anything." He meant the comment as a dig. A reminder of how she'd deceived him so long ago.

But she didn't need any reminders. She lived with the guilt every day. She shrugged. "I wouldn't say that. I'm a big sissy when it comes to sunlight. And wooden stakes. And reality TV."

The sudden tension between them seemed to melt and his mouth hinted at a grin. "Whatever happened to sitcom re-runs?"

"You obviously don't have cable. They've got a channel for that. They've got a channel for everything now. Thankfully. Otherwise, how else would we keep up with the times?"

"*Car and Driver.*"

"Excuse me?"

"That's how I keep up with the times. I read a lot of *Car and Driver*. And *Hot Rod*. And *Motorcycle Mania*."

"Maybe I'm dense, but I don't see how that keeps you up on popular culture."

"Then you haven't read an issue. See, the actual machines keep me up on technological changes. And the car girls…" His smile was slow and wicked and fueled with enough innuendo to make her heart stop. "They keep me updated on popular culture."

"How so?"

"Take Daisy, for instance. She was the centerfold in the last issue of *C & D,* along with the latest eco-friendly Porsche that just rolled off the assembly line. She was wearing a recycled string bikini and sipping a fruit smoothie. One glance at her and I knew green was in."

"One glance at the *TV Guide,* and you'd know that. There are at least a dozen recycling shows on and QVC has an entire hour dedicated to environmentally friendly cosmetics. And neither contributes to the exploitation of women," she added.

"If I didn't know better, I'd say you were jealous." His grin widened. "But then vampires don't get jealous any more than they get scared."

It wasn't a dig this time. Just a simple fact that reminded her that no matter how much she wanted

Garret, she didn't like him. Not genuine, 'til-death-do-us-part like. Maybe a long, long time ago. But even then it hadn't been the real thing. There'd been too many lies between them for the emotion to have been genuine.

She dismissed the strange jealousy niggling at her and said, "I can see how *Car & Driver* would have its benefit for someone in your line of work."

"I don't get a chance to watch much TV, so it's the magazines or nothing else. I stay pretty busy with my choppers."

She eyed the motorcycle skeleton sitting atop the center table. "New project?"

He nodded. "Just one of a dozen on the schedule for this week."

"Sounds like business is good."

"Very. We've got this new software that saves us not only money, but time—"

"Wait." She motioned to him before reaching for her purse. She retrieved a small, hand-held tape recorder from her bag and tried to ignore the hunger yawning inside. Punching the record button, she set the device off to the side. "In case I miss something."

While the article was just a cover to get her here with him, she was still responsible for turning something in to the travel mag who'd fronted her the money for her trip south.

She motioned to him. "Go on."

"We can design, build and finalize a bike in a third the time it used to take."

"We?"

"Jake McCann, Dillon Cash and yours truly. Jake does the design, I do the actual fabrication and Dillon handles overall operations. We don't just handcraft made-to-order custom bikes," he went on, "we're also doing several spec choppers. They're selling like crazy, and so we're getting busier by the minute. This is one of a dozen we're doing for a bike shop in Austin." He hit a button on a nearby computer screen and a 3-D image appeared. "This is what it will look like on completion." Another few buttons and the layers of the bike started to peel away. "This is where we are right now."

"Seems pretty high-tech."

"It is. At the same time, it's still good old-fashioned hard work that makes each bike come to life. We shape everything by hand. The computer software just gives us accurate specs and a list of supplies so that we don't make any costly mistakes along the way." He eyed the recorder. "You sure you want to hear this stuff? I can't imagine you'll include it in a travel article."

"Maybe not, but it gives me an overall handle on the business, which will help with the writing." Hey, it sounded good. Besides, she liked hearing him talk. That had attracted her to him almost as much as the sex. He'd never been one of those men to roll over and fall asleep. He'd pulled her closer into the crook of his arm, rested his head atop hers and talked. About any and everything. About nothing.

She missed his voice almost as much as she missed the toe-curling orgasms.

Almost.

"I need as much information as possible when I write," she went on. "Even information I might not end up using. So how long have you been working with Dillon and Jake?"

The easy rapport they'd lapsed into seemed to melt away, and the tension pushed back in. He grew wary, as if he didn't like her bringing up his coworkers.

He didn't. She could see the hesitation in his gaze, the tensing of his muscles as he fortified his guard.

She didn't think he would answer her, but finally he murmured, "Dillon just came on board about six months ago. He's a local."

"A vampire?"

"Now."

She wanted to ask what that meant, but the dangerous gleam in his gaze warned her off. "What about Jake?"

"We've been friends since the eighteen hundreds."

Which meant he was a vampire, as well.

She wondered if Garret had turned him or if they'd merely banded together as a means of survival. She opened her mouth to ask, but she didn't get the chance.

"I've really got a lot of work to do." His expression closed. "The others will be in later if you have any questions for them. There are several choppers in the holding room." He pointed to a nearby door. "That's where we keep the finished bikes that are waiting to be shipped out. Feel free to set up in there and take as many pictures as you need."

Before she could protest, he pulled on a welding mask, fired up his unit and went to work on the strips of metal sitting on the opposite table.

So much for small talk.

9

VIV SPENT THE NEXT half hour snapping pictures of the various choppers in the holding room. She made sure to leave the door open so she could get in the occasional sultry smile if Garret should happen to glance her way.

He didn't.

No hungry glances. No I-want-you-but-I-don't-want-to-want-you smiles. No I'm-a-sex-starved-vampire-and-I-can't-control-myself stares.

Nada.

"It's not working," she told Winona a few minutes later when she retreated into the ladies room and pulled out her cell phone.

"Who is this?" asked a groggy voice.

"Viv. Viv Darland. The reporter staying at the motel. I sat in on your class tonight." Winona mumbled a groggy "Oh, yeah," and Viv rushed on, "I'm sorry to call so late, but I didn't know what else to do. You said you were available for dating emergencies."

Bedsprings groaned in the background, followed by a faint click as a light switched on. "Are you on a date?" Winona went from groggy to excited in a nanosecond.

"No. I mean, yes. I mean, I'm here and he's here and we're alone, so I guess that qualifies."

"I'm in bed with my cat, Pumpkin, but that doesn't make him my significant other. Scoot, Pumpkin," the woman ordered. "Can't you see I'm working?" Sheets rustled, and a frantic meow echoed in the distance. "Does this man even know you like him?" Winona's attention shifted back to Viv.

She thought of Garret's knowing expression when he'd first walked in on her. The glimmer in his eyes. The sexy murmur of his voice. "Maybe. I'm not really sure."

"Does he like you?"

"I'm not sure about that either. I followed the commandments, but they don't seem to be working. He's ignoring me."

"Maybe he's just trying to come off like he's ignoring you."

"You really think so?"

"That depends. What's he doing right now?"

"Welding."

"All right, so he's ignoring you. But that doesn't mean the commandments aren't working," Winona rushed on as if sensing Viv's disappointment. "It just means you haven't been using them long enough. Just hang in there, and stick to what I taught you. He'll come around eventually."

"The eventually is what I'm afraid of. I don't exactly have a lot of time."

"I know. Eldin told me that as soon as you're finished

with your article, you're moving on. The life of a reporter ain't really conducive to a relationship, is it?"

"No, ma'am." Which was exactly why Viv had chosen it. It kept her moving. Running.

Not anymore.

She swallowed back the sudden lump in her throat. "I would really appreciate any advice you could give me to speed things along."

"Let's see…" Winona seemed to think. "You might try dropping a few knick-knacks. That always worked with my dear, departed husband."

"Knick-knacks?"

"You know, anything. Everything. The point is to give him an eyeful when you go to pick up whatever it is you dropped. Either it's an eyeful of cleavage or your ba-donk-a-donk. Why, I was bent over cleaning dust bunnies out from under the fridge when my oldest daughter was conceived. Can't get a better success rate than that."

"Thanks."

"Thank you. I charge extra for on-call. I'll drop a bill by your motel room first thing tomorrow morning." A loud click punctuated the statement.

Viv dropped her cell back into her purse, splashed some cold water onto her face and summoned her courage. She walked back into the large room where she'd set up her equipment and slid a glance toward the open doorway that led to the fabrication shop.

Garret wore heat-resistant gloves that went clear to his elbows. A welding mask hid his face as he torched the edge of a metal strip before hammering it down.

Torch. Hammer. Torch. Hammer.

She fought down a wave of self-consciousness and reached for a roll of film. After plucking the package from her equipment bag, she half-turned. Her fingers went limp, and the roll hit the concrete with a soft thud.

"Oh, no. Clumsy me," she said, her voice a few decibals louder than normal. She gathered her determination, bent at the waist and did a slow motion retrieval that would have perpetuated the Adkins gene pool for the next fifty years.

Just as her fingers closed around the film, she stalled for a few seconds to give Garret an eyeful.

He didn't spare her a glance.

Instead, he bent over the metal, his attention fully focused on his task.

Torch. Hammer. Torch. Hammer.

Her gaze snagged on one bicep and the familiar slave band tattoo that peeked beneath the edge. The sight reminded her of her own markings, and guilt spiraled through her followed by a wave of self-doubt.

Maybe he was really and truly no longer attracted to her. Despite the hunger that lived and breathed inside of him.

Because of it.

Because he could satisfy his need with any woman. Every woman. He didn't need her. Not emotionally or physically. He never had. He'd just been mesmerized.

Her chest tightened at the thought.

Not that it mattered.

All that really mattered was that she needed him.

While he could get what he craved from any female, she could only get what she so desperately wanted—a bona fide orgasm—from one male.

Him.

If she really wanted to orgasm with an actual partner, she couldn't let herself get discouraged.

She wiggled just a little to emphasize her breasts before she straightened and put the film back into her bag. Her hand brushed the lens cap sitting on the table, and it tumbled over the edge.

"Whoops," she said again. Louder this time. "I swear I'm all thumbs tonight."

If at first you don't succeed. . .

IF SHE DROPPED ONE more thing—anything—he was going to stake himself with the nearest sharp object.

That is, if he didn't burst into a ball of flames first.

He hit the Off switch on the welder, and the blue flame died. But it did nothing to ease the fire that burned inside of him.

He was too worked up.

Too turned on.

Too damned intent on retaining his control and keeping the hunger contained.

Lust pushed and pulled inside of him. His nerves buzzed. Electricity sizzled across his skin, and he grew hotter by the second.

He tugged off his T-shirt, but the rush of air against his bare skin did little to help. He reached for a plain sheet of metal. The cool material heated instantly beneath the hot pads of his fingertips. The air seemed to shimmer with the heat radiating from his body.

As if confirming his worst fear, the temperature-sensitive fans near the computer table kicked on with a click and whoosh. They revved, cranking up to full blast to cool down the rapidly warming equipment.

He heard the glub, glub, glub of bubbles. The sharp scent of boiling gasoline spiraled from the half-full gallon-sized container sitting near the doorway.

And all because of her.

Because he wanted her, and he couldn't—wouldn't act on it.

Don't look.

That's what he told himself.

But damned if his eyes would cooperate.

When she leaned over just the way she was doing right now, her backside to him, he couldn't not look.

He caught a glimpse of the dewy pink flesh between her legs. The tender insides of her thighs. The tiny beauty mark that dotted her left ass cheek.

His groin throbbed, and his gut clenched. He felt the sharp graze of his fangs against his tongue. The heat sizzling his fingertips—

Damn it.

His gaze dropped to the smoke spiraling from his grip on the piece of metal. He dropped the material and stared through the shimmering air at his seared black skin.

"Just call me klutz." Her voice slid into his ears and snagged his attention.

He glanced up in time to see the bright blue of her eyes and the fullness of her lips just before she bent forward—facing him this time—to retrieve her lens cap. Her blouse ballooned, and her breasts quivered. He glimpsed one ripe nipple as she shifted and reached.

Every muscle in his body went tight. He balled his fingers against a wave of white-hot need that drenched him. His vision blurred, and his ears started to ring.

Through a haze he saw her straighten. She tugged at the collar of her blouse, as if she felt the heat as much as he did. Her gaze collided with his. Desire brightened her eyes, along with a glimmer of desperation that reached across the distance separating them and sucker-punched him right in the gut.

She made a big show of dropping another roll of film, and Garret reached his limit.

He was halfway across the room, his fangs extended, his heart pounding, his hunger raging, when the gas can exploded.

10

THE NEXT FEW MOMENTS seemed to go in slow motion as the fire blazed from the container's spout, shot up the wall and ate up the door frame.

Viv's expression went from startled to scared as she inched backwards, away from the bright orange waves that now separated them.

The fire alarm sounded, and the overhead sprinklers kicked on.

The cold water hit him, and everything seemed to speed up then. He grabbed a nearby fire extinguisher and rushed forward. White foam spewed, drenching the flames until the last lick of orange fizzled. In a matter of seconds, the wall went from a fiery blaze to a smoldering black mess.

Garret chucked the extinguisher and crossed the threshold. He reached for Viv. "Are you okay?"

She nodded, but he wasn't convinced. Fear brightened her eyes, and his chest tightened. He swept his gaze from her head to her toes and back up again. She was soaked from the sprinklers and still a little freaked out from the sudden fire, but otherwise she looked okay.

His gaze collided with hers, and the strange glimmer seemed to fade into the blue depths. Her eyes glittered, the color shifting, morphing, into a brilliant blaze of purple.

And suddenly she looked more hungry than afraid.

Time seemed to stand still for the next few moments as they stood there staring at each other. The sprinkler rained down on them, cooling off the temperature in the room. But it didn't begin to touch the heat that churned inside of him.

His body tightened and his vision blurred, and he knew his eyes gleamed just as hot, as bright, as wild as hers.

The air sizzled, and steam rose. The water chugged and splattered for several more seconds until the automatic shut-off finally kicked in.

"What just happened?" Her voice, soft and breathless, barely pushed past the frantic beat of his heart.

He licked his lips and gathered his control. "The, um, air conditioner has been acting up." Like hell. But it was the best he could come up with and a damned sight better than the truth—that he wanted to kiss her.

He wouldn't.

No matter how much he suddenly wanted to.

"I guess it finally blew," he added.

His hearing perked and through the sound of dripping water he could hear the steady drone of the central cooling unit.

Judging from the "yeah, right" look on her face, so could she.

"Temporarily," he rushed on. "It must be one of those things that comes and goes. You know, one minute the problem is here, the next it clears itself up."

"Probably." That's what she said, but he could see the doubt in her gaze. He could also see a hell of a lot more thanks to the sprinklers.

Her clothes were soaked. Her silky red shirt plastered to her breasts and outlined her hard, ripe nipples. Water ran in tiny rivulets down her face, her smooth, curved neck, to disappear in the deep V between her luscious breasts. She was soaked, her skin slick and gleaming, and he couldn't help but wonder if she was just as wet between her legs.

He could easily find out. All he had to do was reach out. Hitch up her skirt. Trail his palms over her soft, smooth ass. Plunge his hand between her silky thighs. Dip his fingers into the hot, sweltering folds. Stroke her swollen, throbbing clit.

As if she read the decadent thoughts wreaking havoc on his control, her nostrils flared and her chest hitched. Urgency gleamed in her gaze, and he knew she wanted him to touch her and find out.

If only. But she didn't want him. He could have been any man. He was nothing but a meal ticket to her.

Nothing.

That's what he told himself, but he didn't quite believe it. Not with the two of them standing so close, the air so steamy and hot as they gazed at each other, into each other. While he couldn't read her the way he did a human, he could see the uncertainty in the way she caught her bottom lip and gripped her hands together.

The sight chipped away at his control because Viv Darland didn't feel such things. She was a vampire, for Christ's sake.

Commanding. Determined. Self-assured.

She looked anything but at the moment, and it tied his damned self-control into knots.

That, and he couldn't forget the fear in her eyes. The real, raw fear caused by the fire.

"You should really get that fixed," she told him, as if eager to ease the tension that crackled around them. "The air conditioner, I mean. I would imagine it gets pretty hot in here what with all the equipment."

"Yep, it's definitely an equipment problem."

Her gaze slid past him to the welding unit, the sheet cutter, the shaper. "What with all the stuff in here, the place could go up in flames if you're not careful." She glanced at the ceiling. "But then I guess that's what the sprinklers are for."

"Yes." His gaze dropped to her nipples pressing provocatively against the drenched fabric before shifting back to her face, and suddenly he couldn't help himself.

He reached out.

His fingertip circled one hard tip outlined beneath the wet fabric of her shirt. She hissed and went perfectly still.

"There's nothing like a good sprinkler system to calm things down," he murmured. A few more strokes, and she clamped down on her bottom lip. "Or liven things up."

"I…" She seemed to be fighting hard for her own control. As hard as he'd fought just a few moments ago. But the battle was futile. The pull between them was too fierce. Too compelling. And suddenly it was all he could think of.

His gaze collided with hers. "You look good wet," he murmured, and then he pulled her into his arms.

GARRET SAWYER had lived and breathed in Viv's memory for so long. The feel of his hard, hot body pressed against hers, his arms locked tight, his lips eating at hers. But the memories were nothing compared to the real thing.

Electricity skimmed her skin and heat firebombed the pit of her stomach as he drew her close.

Closer.

His hands spanned her waist, slid over her ass and cupped the round fullness. He pulled her flush against him and lifted her. Her legs came around him, and he hoisted her, sliding her up the hard ridge of his erection until he was eye-level with her chest. His tongue flicked out, and she barely caught the moan that worked its way up her throat.

Heat licked the tip of her nipple, and a burst of pleasure zapped her brain. She bowed toward him.

He touched her with his tongue again and licked her longer, more leisurely, savoring the ripeness of her. She gasped and clung to him.

His lips closed over her nipple. The wet material of her shirt provided little protection against the searing inferno of his mouth. Heat surrounded her areola as he drew on her, sucking long and hard.

She threaded her fingers through his hair, tilted her head back and gave herself up to sensation.

The pressure of his mouth increased. His tongue stroked. His lips suckled. Each pull on her nipple sent an echoing tug between her legs. She clutched at his bare shoulders, desperate to relieve the pressure building inside of her.

It was coming. She could feel it.

His hands held her steady, scorching her as he nestled her crotch against the ripped hardness of his abdomen.

Then he moved her, a frantic brush of her sex up and down the muscled ridges, and the pressure neared maximum intensity. She was so close.

Too close.

As wonderful as it was, it wasn't what she wanted.

She wanted him inside of her when she went over the edge. She needed it.

Stop!

The command echoed through her head, and her fingers tightened in his hair. But instead of pushing him away, she couldn't help herself. She pulled him closer and rubbed herself against him and…there. And there. And, oh, yes, there.

She felt the waistband of his jeans rasp her slit, the metal of his button a cold shock against her ultra-sensitive clitoris, and a lightning bolt went through her. Her nerves tingled, and the sharp edge of her fangs pressed against her tongue.

Desperation rushed through her, and she lifted herself for another slide and shimmy. He stopped her cold, his arms tightening in a grip that rendered her immobile.

Her eyes popped open to see a fierce look on his face. His grip tightened for a split-second before it loosened and her feet hit the floor.

The next few moments passed in a dizzying blur. One minute they were pressed against each other, and the next she was standing alone as Garret threw open a small storage unit on the opposite side of the room.

A heartbeat later, he was back. He tossed a Skull Creek Choppers T-shirt around her shoulders. Large hands tugged her wet skirt down around her hips just as the outer doorway opened and two couples filed into the adjoining office.

They were laughing and talking and then bam, four pairs of eyes stared through the wall of windows and fixated on her. Everyone went silent.

Viv gathered the extra large tee around her and tried to control her frantic heartbeat.

But Garret was still too close, his hard body just to her right. In her peripheral vision she could see him wipe his drenched face with a second T-shirt before scrubbing at his hair. Her skin still burned where his fingers had rubbed her thighs as he'd tugged the skirt down to a respectable level.

The hunger raged, urging her to turn and reach for him. To beg for his touch all over her body and finish what they'd started regardless of the audience.

But it was too late.

While he stood only inches away physically, emotionally he'd already traveled a few hundred miles.

Gone was the desire that had brightened his eyes. Ice blue chips glittered back at her when she chanced a glance at him. Regret glimmered in the translucent depths and her chest tightened.

She blinked against the sudden burning in her own eyes. "I—I really should be going."

"Yeah."

"I'll finish up tomorrow night after everything dries out." She snatched up her soaked camera bag. "I'll need to pick up some new lighting equipment. Is it all right if I leave all the wet stuff here for now?"

Without waiting for a reply, she sailed past him and pushed through the nearest side door marked Exit. She didn't slow down until she reached the opposite side of the small parking lot where her car was parked.

She stalled for a few seconds and drank in a heavy draft of air.

As if that would help.

She climbed behind the wheel, keyed the ignition and revved the engine.

The roar did little to drown out the sound of his heartbeat that echoed in her ears and followed her as she turned out onto Main Street. Along with the voice that whispered in her ear.

"It's not happening between us."

She knew then that while she'd won the battle tonight, she wasn't even close to winning the war. He had no intention of having sex with her no matter how much he wanted her.

Or how much she wanted him.

"Never, ever again."

His deep voice followed, whispering in her ear, stirring her insecurity and her doubt.

She shouldn't have come here.

She wouldn't have if she could just forget.

The feel of his arms, his hands, his lips…

Her body tingled, and heat spiraled through her. No, she couldn't forget. And while he might regret what had just happened, the point was, it had happened.

Which meant that it could happen again.

Garret would lose control, they would go all the way, and she would get one more chance to experience the earth-shattering orgasm that had eluded her since she'd walked away from him all those years ago.

That's all she wanted from him, she reminded herself. She certainly didn't want him to need her. To like her.

This was all about sex.

Breath-stealing, toe-curling, bone-melting sex.

At least that's what she told herself as she headed back to the motel.

11

"YOU'VE BEEN HOLDING out on us." Jake stared at the Exit door where Viv had just disappeared.

Garret shook his head. "It's not like that, man."

"Isn't it?" Jake arched an eyebrow and gave Garret a knowing look. Not because he'd actually witnessed the wet and wild bump and grind.

He hadn't.

Garret had felt his fellow vampires long before they'd keyed in the security code and opened the outer doorway.

No, Jake knew because of Garret.

Because he was staring at him right now, and he could see the brightness that lingered in his gaze. The tension in his body. The hunger that radiated from him, along with a shimmer of heat. He wasn't anywhere close to starting another fire thanks to the douse of water and the arrival of his friends, but he was still worked up.

"Who is she?" Jake asked.

"A freelance reporter." When Jake didn't look the least bit satisfied, Garret shrugged. "Just somebody I used to know. A long, long time ago."

"Vampire?" The question came from Nikki. Her lips hinted at a grin and curiosity danced in her excited expression. Garret nodded and she added, "No wonder you're not interested in a fix-up. Donna Sue's got a pretty big dose of sex appeal and can give the hotties in this town a run for their money, but she doesn't have anything close to vamp charisma."

"So you like this woman?" It was Meg's turn.

"No." Like didn't begin to touch what he felt for Viv Darland.

Disappointment? Definitely.

Resentment? Ditto.

Fear? A little.

Lust? A shitload.

But that was it.

Nothing else. Nothing powerful.

He ignored the small voice that insisted otherwise and shifted his attention to Dillon.

The younger vampire stared at the Exit door before his gaze slid back to Garret. You are so busted gleamed loud and clear. The younger vamp opened his mouth for confirmation, but Garret spoke first.

"Don't ask."

Dillon shrugged. "Hey, your sex life is your own business."

"They didn't have sex." Meg nudged him. Excitement lit her face and her eyes swiveled to Nikki. "Did they?"

Nikki looked at Jake. "Honey?"

"Garret?" Jake arched an eyebrow.

"I'm out of here." Garret turned and reached for his keys.

"We'll take that as a yes," Nikki's amused voice followed him to the doorway.

"A big fat yes," Meg added.

If only.

Garret shook off a pang of disappointment. He wasn't having sex with Viv Darland. He wasn't.

His head knew that, but his damned body didn't seem to be getting the message.

His groin throbbed, and his muscles ached. Hunger twisted at his insides, fighting and clawing for sustenance.

He tamped down on the urge to find the nearest woman and end the torment eating away at him. He could, but that would mean breaking his vow, and he wasn't about to do that.

He'd held out this long, and he wasn't caving now. No sex. Not with Viv. Not with any woman.

Not until he'd reclaimed his humanity.

In the meantime, Garret did what he'd been doing for the past few months when the need grew too great. He headed home to chug a few bags of blood and climb into an ice-cold shower.

"DO YOU ALWAYS wear a suit and tie when you deliver extra towels?" Viv asked when she arrived at the motel to find Eldin waiting on her doorstep.

He wore a pin-striped navy suit, a red dress shirt, red tennis shoes and a wide smile. "It's part of our first-class treatment here at the Skull Creek Inn." He handed her a fluffy stack of folded white cotton and stepped back while she slid her key card into the slot and unlocked the door. "That, and I like to be ready for any late night dating opportunities." The door opened, and he followed her inside. "You can quote me on that."

"Will do." Viv set the towels on a nearby table and moved to close the door.

Eldin didn't budge. Instead, he stood rooted just inside the doorway, an expectant look on his face.

Realization dawned and she shrugged. "I can't take any pictures tonight. I lost most of my film in a freak fire over at the chopper shop." Okay, so that wasn't the complete truth. While she had, indeed, lost the rolls she'd had with her, she kept an extra stash in the trunk of her car, along with two back-up digital cameras. But the last thing she wanted was to spend the next fifteen minutes taking pics of Eldin. She was too worked up— too hot—and she needed a cold shower in the worst way. "The inside sprinklers came on and ruined everything." She indicated her damp clothes.

As if noticing them for the first time, he nodded. "You're all wet."

"And so is my film. I'll have to pick more up at the pharmacy tomorrow."

"Just write down what you need, and I'll fetch it for you first thing in the morning."

"I couldn't put you to so much trouble."

"No trouble at all. Just part of our VIP Ultra-Deluxe vacation package which also includes free muffins, a

Buy-One-Get-One-Free entrée coupon for Little Pigs Barbecue just a spit and holler down the road and an unlimited supply of Tums. You'll need it after eating the ribs." He pulled a folded sheet of paper from his pocket. "This outlines all the different packages we offer, and it also includes the itinerary for the vacation I'm taking this summer."

Viv scanned the page. "You're taking a couples cruise? I thought you were single?"

"At the moment, but I'm hoping your article can hook me up before I sail. I prefer a blonde, but at this point I'm willing to look at most anyone who might be interested. You can quote me on that, too."

"Um, yeah." Viv grabbed the door. "I'd really like to get out of these wet clothes."

Eldin still didn't budge. "How you doin' on ice? You need another bucketful before bedtime?"

"I'm good." She stepped forward, urging him back a few inches.

"Complimentary soap?"

"I'm still working on the six extra bars you left yesterday." She took another step, but he stalled in the threshold and she added, "They really work up a good lather."

"They should for what I'm paying Marvin over at the pharmacy. He says I ought to order the stuff in gross if I want a discount."

"Sounds like a plan."

"Shower cap? I'd be happy to fetch you another."

"The one I have is still working like a champ." She

stared deep into his eyes and sent a silent message. Go. He backed up, and she moved to close the door. The minute their gazes disconnected, however, his hand shot through the crack to grip the doorjamb.

"If you need anything else, you know who to call. Me. Eldin. That's E-L-D-I-N. Some folks spell it with two Es, but my parents wanted something unique."

"I'll make a note of that."

The hand loosened from the doorjamb only to tighten again. "Oh, I almost forgot. You had a couple of phone calls."

Viv opened the door a few inches. "Who?"

"One was a Cindy Marsfield with Southern Travel. She said her assistant lost your cell number. Since we're not set up for voicemail here, she asked if I could relay a message. She said they moved up your deadline. It's two weeks from today."

Viv nodded. She'd planned on turning it in to Cindy sooner anyway because she knew the odds were that Cruz and Molly would find her before then, and she didn't want any loose ends left hanging. Cindy had given her the job that had led her back to Garret. She owed the woman.

Article? Check.

Orgasm? Check, check.

At least that had been the plan.

"Never, ever again."

Garret's deep voice echoed in her ears, and she focused her attention on Eldin. Anything to ignore the doubt that gripped her.

"What about the other calls?"

"There was just one." He shrugged. "Don't know who it was. The man didn't leave a message. He just asked if I had a Viviana Darland registered here and what room she was in." He must have noticed the sudden stiffening of Viv's body, because he rushed on, "But don't worry. I didn't give you up. If there's one thing we pride ourselves on here at the Skull Creek, it's protecting the privacy of each and every celebrity guest. Why, we had Norm Shannon here last year, and not so much as one groupie wiggled past yours truly."

"Norm Shannon?"

"He hosts a local AM radio show. He does cow impersonations," he added, as if that explained it all. "The FFA kids over at the high school just love him. He was in town to speak at their annual banquet, and he was really worried that he wouldn't be able to get a decent night's rest on account of his ratings recently tripled— he started doing chickens in addition to the cows. But I sat in the parking lot with my BB gun and made sure none of them youngsters got within twenty feet of him. I didn't have to shoot anybody, mind you. The darned thing wasn't even loaded. It was more of a bluff than anything else, but it worked like a charm. So don't you worry a bit. If anyone tries to bother you while you're here, I'll deal with them. I know you famous writer types like to keep a low profile."

Writing articles for a sleazy tabloid hardly qualified her for celebrity status, but she appreciated Eldin's protective instincts all the same.

Not that a BB gun would be of any use against Cruz and Molly. They wanted their humanity back, and they wouldn't stop until Viv was dead for good this time.

Time.

The word lingered in her mind as she closed and locked the door behind Eldin and tried to shake the tingling awareness that gripped every inch of her.

The same awareness she'd felt walking down that mountain, away from the site of the Butcher's latest bloodbath, with Sheriff Matt Keller.

She'd known then that Cruz and Molly were close.

Just as she knew now.

The truth closed in on her, and she trembled.

While they were just calling around right now, checking facts, it wouldn't be long before they got enough confirmation to draw them here in person. It would be just a matter of days—if that long—before they finally showed up for a repeat of the Washington ambush.

She turned on the cold water and peeled off her shirt. Anxiety gripped her body, along with frustration.

Her gut clenched, and hunger gnawed at her. Her hands trembled, and her nipples throbbed.

She ignored the doubt that nibbled away at her determination and focused on analyzing the evening and what had driven Garret over the edge.

He'd managed to resist her while they were in different rooms, but when the fire started he'd come to her rescue. Face-to-face, with the heat burning between them, he'd been unable to hold back.

Close.

That was the key. All she had to do was stick to him like glue, and they would be doing the nasty in no time.

She clung to the hope, shimmied off her skirt and stepped beneath the icy spray.

_12_

DISTANCE.

That was the key to resisting Viv and keeping his fire insurance coverage from going through the friggin' roof.

Garret tossed another hay bale from the bed of the 4 x 4 Chevy pick-up. It landed in a pile near the three others he'd already unloaded. He jumped down off the tailgate. One hand dove into his back pocket and retrieved a pair of wire cutters.

He snipped the tie on each bale before climbing back into the cab. He gunned the engine and headed for the adjacent pasture to drop off the last bale for the handful of broncing bucks he'd purchased last week.

He'd yet to turn them out with the rest of his herd. He wouldn't until they were broken.

If they were broken.

When he'd been just a man, he'd been able to tame the wildest horse. But now... Now he couldn't get within fifty feet. The horses saw his true nature, and they feared it.

He didn't blame them. He would have pissed himself

if he'd known who—what—Viviana really was when he'd first met her. And he sure as hell wouldn't have put his trust in her.

Her image popped into his head, and he saw her the way she'd looked on that first night. Her luscious body clad in white cotton bloomers, her cleavage pushing up from an ultra-tight corset, her long dark hair flowing down around her shoulders. She'd been beautiful. Mesmerizing. Irresistible.

Then and now.

Only the circumstances were different now. He didn't want her because of what she was. He wanted her because of what he was. Because he'd been mainly bagging it since he'd come to Skull Creek, and he was desperate for the real thing.

Blood and sex.

His muscles tightened, and his gut clenched as he snipped the wire on the last bale. He'd been cold turkey for so long, and he was starting to feel it. That was the reason for his temporary loss of control tonight. A loss that wouldn't have occurred if he hadn't been in a confined space with her.

He ignored the tiny voice that whispered there was nothing confining about a massive fabrication shop with three spacious bays and twenty-foot ceilings.

He needed distance. Space.

His nerves twitched, and his gaze shifted to the faint orange line outlining the distant trees.

Forget space. What he needed at the moment was to get the hell out of here before sunup. Already he could feel the heat creeping toward him and smell the sunshine hiding just behind the cluster of oak trees.

His skin tingled, and his hands clinched.

As anxious as he was, there was a small part of him that refused to hurry. He couldn't help but wonder if the sun still felt as warm, as honest as it once had so long ago.

It did. He knew it. It was a certainty that grew stronger with each day that passed since he'd moved to Skull Creek, Texas.

Moved, but not settled.

No, Garret Sawyer was still very much unsettled. Still restless. Still waiting.

For the chance to breathe again, to feel, to live.

He shifted his attention back to the cutters in his hand. A quick snip, and the wires popped. He lifted the bale and scattered it for several feet.

He could have easily paid someone to do the work for him. Or even bought one of those state-of-the-art balers that could cut and drop in a fifth the time it took him to load his truck and do the job himself.

He had the money thanks to the success of his choppers.

But it felt good to get his hands dirty.

Normal.

The thought struck and he pushed it away. He was anything but, and he had a burnt mess back at his shop to prove it.

No, he wasn't normal.

He might never be normal again. He saw the proof

in the glittering black eyes of the nearest horse. Delilah. The rich, sweet smell of hay filled the air, and her nostrils flared. She took a few steps toward him, only to draw up short several feet away.

Garret walked back to the cab and pulled a bag of apple slices from the dashboard. He pulled out a slice and held it out to her. The animal drew another step closer, her nose twitching, her hunger battling with her survival instincts.

A knowing light gleamed in her eyes as she stared at Garret.

"It's okay," he murmured, but the animal wasn't the least bit fooled.

Garret's fingers itched to cross the space between them and stroke the animal's soft fur. It had been so long since he'd felt the silky horsehair.

Too long.

He knelt and set the apple slice on the ground, and then he turned and climbed back into the truck. Behind the wheel, he pulled out his cell and thumbed through his messages.

He had three, but none of them were from Dalton McGregor. Not that he'd expected one this soon. The man had given him a respectable timetable, and Garret had done enough reference checks to know that he kept his word. By Saturday MacGregor would have the information Garret so desperately needed to reclaim his humanity.

Two days, he reminded himself. Two days, and he would be one step closer to the man he'd once been.

The notion didn't excite him half as much as the thought of seeing Viv again.

Understandable, of course. He was so damned hungry, so fucking desperate for a woman, that he couldn't think straight. It wasn't her.

It never had been.

The hunger clawed inside of him, and his fingers went stiff as he pocketed the cell phone. All he had to do was head for the interstate and the nearest bar. He could take his pick of any woman there and forget all about Viv Darland.

He shifted the pick-up into gear, gunned the engine and headed for the far gate. Once out on the main road, he idled for a split-second, indecision pushing and pulling inside of him. Finally, he hung a right onto the dirt trail that led back to the ranch house.

As much as he hurt, he wasn't acting on it. He didn't have time. The sun was already creeping over the horizon which meant he was bagging it today.

And tomorrow.

And the next day.

Because he'd made a promise to himself. One he didn't intend to break, no matter how hungry Viv made him.

The next time Garret climbed into bed with a woman, it would be because he wanted to. Not because he had to. Because he craved the feel of her body and the smell of her skin and the dizzying energy as she came apart in his arms.

An image slid into his head, and his stomach muscles

bunched. Heat spiraled through him, making him harder and hotter.

He cranked up the air conditioner, gathered his resolve and forced Viv out of his head.

He was keeping his priorities straight and his distance where she was concerned. Even more, he wasn't getting stuck under the same roof with her while she leaned this way and bent that way and worked him into a sexually frustrated frenzy.

Never, ever again.

"FORGET THE EQUIPMENT BAG," Garret said when he met Viv in the parking lot of Skull Creek Choppers on Wednesday evening. "We're traveling light."

Viv eyed the black and silver motorcycle with the skull and crossbones motif that now sat parked near the doorway. "A ride?"

"A road trip. I've got to test out this bike and make sure she performs up to spec before I send her out. The only way to do that is to take her out and open her up."

Excitement flared in her gaze for a split-second before she seemed to tamp down on it long enough to give him a calm, controlled, "Sounds good." She pulled out her camera before tossing her bag into the car, then slammed and locked the door. "So," she said, turning back to the bike and hooking the camera strap over her shoulder. "How do we do this? Do I get on first or last?"

"First."

When she started to straddle the chopper, he caught

her arm. Skin met skin and the air around them seemed to crackle. She stalled, and her gaze locked with his. For just the smallest moment, the past seemed to fade. The hurt. The betrayal.

Suddenly it was just the two of them standing beneath the stars, staring into each other's eyes the way they'd done so long ago.

When he'd been a man, and she'd been just a woman.

Or so he'd thought.

He stiffened and let his hand fall away. "Not that one." He pointed to another chopper parked a few feet away near the back door. It was a silver and pink number he'd just completed for a runway model from New York. "That one. I'm shipping it out next week, and I want to do some final tweaks. You're about the same size as the client, so you can give me a feel for how she'll handle."

"But I can't ride." For a split-second, there was more than simply dismay in her gaze. He saw a glimmer of uncertainty. Fear. And something softened inside of him.

"You can ride a horse, can't you?"

"Sure. About a hundred years ago before I grew vampire cooties."

A smile tugged at his lips. "It doesn't matter. Once you've done it, you never forget how. Just stash your camera in that compartment beneath the seat, climb on, keep your knees locked and your hands steady, and you'll be fine."

She looked hesitant, but finally she walked over, stashed her camera and straddled the bike. Her fingers tightened on the hand grips. "I hope you have good insurance."

"Why's that?"

"Because if I fall off this thing, I'm going to sue." When he started to remind her that her injuries would heal faster than he could call 911 or pull out a first aid kit, she added, "For the emotional duress I'm going to suffer when I fall on my ass in front of everyone and make a complete idiot of myself."

"We're taking the backroads, so the only one likely to see you on your ass will be me. I've busted my own more than once, so you'll be in good company."

She looked doubtful. "You've really fallen off one of these things?"

"One or two times." He shrugged. "Or forty-three."

"You're not making me feel any better." She eyed him.

"I was popping wheelies or racing or doing something equally stupid when I bit the dust. You won't have that problem because we're going to go nice and slow."

She eyed the bike again, and disappointment glimmered before diving into the deep blue depths of her eyes. "I guess I don't really have a choice, do I? If I want to ride, it's this or nothing."

"This or you can take pictures inside and wait for Jake and Dillon. I'm sure one of them would double up and give you a tour of the town when they come in."

"But not you?"

"I've got my own bike to evaluate. I need an accurate

ride," he added, suddenly eager to convince himself. "Two people throw the balance off. I need to make shock and alignment adjustments. If you climb on, my readings will be messed up." And so would his control.

Already, he could feel his body temperature rising. His hands trembled, and it was all he could do not to reach out and pull her close.

He wanted to taste her again.

To feel her.

"I'm crunched for time on this. The bike has to go out tomorrow."

She sat there for a long moment as if trying to make up her mind. Stay or go. With him or without him. "It's heavier than it looks," she finally said, turning the handlebars from side to side.

"Only because it's stationary. Once we start moving, she'll loosen up."

Indecision faded into serious intent. "I really could use some firsthand experience," she admitted. Then, eyeing the bike as if she were a bullfighter about to climb into the ring, she asked, "What do I do first?"

13

IT WAS NOTHING like riding a horse.

The cold metal against the insides of her bare knees. The hot exhaust blowing around her ankles. The soft, cushiony seat pillowing her bottom. The steady vibration between her legs.

A horse wasn't nearly this exciting.

This stirring.

This decadent.

The wind whipped at her face and lifted the neckline of her blouse. Air teased her nipples, stirring them to a full, throbbing awareness. Electricity rippled up her spine and she chanced a glance to the side to see Garret staring back at her.

Again.

As reassuring as he'd been about her ability to ride, he seemed intent on keeping a close eye on her.

A strange warmth blossomed in her chest. A crazy feeling because the last thing she wanted from him was his concern.

Her nipples pebbled, and she shifted on the seat. A bad move even though she'd worn panties tonight. They were thin enough to be non-existent, and desire spurted through her, along with a rush of anxiety.

"How much longer until we get where we're going?" she asked. Where the wind would have masked her voice to the normal human, Garret heard her loud and clear.

"It's not about getting somewhere. It's about the ride, sugar. Just relax."

Sugar.

The sentiment stuck in her head, and the warmth spread from her chest throughout the rest of her body. Need spiraled through her, dive-bombing several erogenous zones and making her that much more uncomfortable. And desperate.

She tightened her grip on the handlebars and did her damndest not to shift on the seat. No problem when they were on the main highway. But when Garret turned off onto an old dirt path, Viv knew she was in big trouble.

Sure enough, she bounced this way and slid that way and rubbed up and down and—

Easy.

Yeah, right. By the time they came to a stop by the edge of a sprawling river, she was this close to going up in flames.

She killed the engine and sat there for a few seconds trying to gather her control. Just one teensy, tiny move and she was going to—

She bit down on her bottom lip and fought back the burst of dizzying pleasure. Her vision clouded, and she clamped her eyes shut. Her ears rang. She could feel her fangs sharp against her tongue. Her hands tightened on the handlebars, and she braced herself.

Not yet. Not like—

"Are you okay?"

Garret's voice pushed past the roar in her head, and she forced her eyes open to find him staring back at her.

He sat a few feet away on the black and chrome chopper. His hands rested atop his thighs. He looked as relaxed as ever except for the tense set to his jaw. As if he knew the turmoil her body was caught in, and it took all of his strength not to climb off the motorcycle and help her out.

"I…" She swallowed against the tightness in her throat and summoned her control. "I'm just feeling a little dizzy. It was a rough ride." And not nearly satisfying enough. "I… Just let me sit here for a minute and catch my bearings."

She waited for him to remind her that she was a vampire who wasn't susceptible to motion sickness. She could leap tall buildings and levitate and walk on water, for Pete's sake. Motion sickness? Forget about it.

He didn't say a word. Instead, he gave her a thoughtful look before he finally shrugged and climbed off the bike.

He walked over to the edge of the water and hunkered down. Pulling out a shiny black PDA, he started keying in notes. He seemed oblivious to Viv, and she sent up a silent thank-you.

She spent the next few minutes telling herself every reason why she shouldn't climb off the bike, march over to him and jump his bones.

Slow, she reminded herself. Easy. She needed him to be the aggressor. That's why she'd had an orgasm in the first place. Because he'd seduced her. He'd turned the tables on her and taken control. That's what had sent her over the edge.

If she took the lead, she wouldn't be any more satisfied than she'd been with any other man. She had to wait on him.

She eyed his broad back outlined by the moonlight reflecting off the calm water. Her tummy tingled and her knees shook and desperation coiled low in her belly.

No, she wasn't going to jump him.

At the same time, she wasn't going to sit here and just wait. She had to do something.

"Shimmy, shake, shazam." Winona's crackling voice echoed through her head.

It had been the woman's last piece of advice when Viv had called her on the way to Skull Creek Choppers that evening.

"If the drop and retrieve didn't send him over the edge, you have to get more aggressive. You got to send a crystal-clear message that says you're ready for sex, and nothing does that better than stripping buck naked smack dab in front of him."

"Isn't that a little too aggressive?"

"Not if you don't say the words. See, telling a man you want to have sex with him takes all the guesswork out of it, which takes away the challenge. Every man wants what he can't have. So the key here is to let him see what it is he can't have. Sort of like dangling the carrot in front of him. Then when he makes like Bugs Bunny and tries to grab you, you back off."

"Why would I back off if he tries to grab me?"

"'Cause you're dangling, darlin'. Trust me, if you strip naked and employ my infamous Triple S, he'll make another move. And then another. My rule of thumb is three moves minimum. Then you can give in. Just remember to shimmy and shake every time you take off something."

"What about the shazam? How do I do that?"

"It's not something you do, darlin'." The old woman laughed. "That's what happens when that man finally gets ahold of you. Shazam!"

Viv gathered her courage and turned on the state-of-the-art sound system built into the chopper's dash. A frantic heavy metal song blasted from the speakers, and she punched the buttons until she found a soft, slow country song with just enough beat for what she had in mind.

She climbed off the bike. "Nice sound system," she commented. "Is it standard on all your bikes?"

"We don't have a 'standard.' We cater to each customer." He didn't spare her a glance. "Some want more power than others. Some want CD only. Some want XM. Some want it all. We give them what they want."

"It's nice." She fingered the edge of the red sequined tank top she'd bought today just minutes before the boutique had closed. Actually, they'd already turned off the sign, but she'd used her persuasive gaze to get the salesclerk to open up for one final purchase—a blue jean mini-skirt, strappy tank and a pair of killer red heels. "So, um, how did your bike handle?"

"Fine, with the exception of a few suspension problems. But they're easy to fix." He still didn't turn her way.

"So," she came up next to him on the riverbank, "where exactly are we?"

"The river."

"I know that. What river?"

"It's really deep, so the folks around here call it the Bottomless Pit."

"That sort of kills the mood."

A warm chuckle vibrated on the air. "Black Bottom River is the official name."

"Oh." She went silent for a few moments as the night's sounds closed in on her. The occasional hooting of an owl, the faint ripple of water, the click of his fingers on the PDA, the distant drone of the highway miles away. Wind rippled, sneaking beneath the edge of her skirt to tickle her thighs and the tender flesh between her legs.

She shifted. "Garret?"

"Yeah?"

"Could you look here for a second? I've got something to show you."

He didn't budge. "I really need to finish these adjustments for the suspension system in case I forget something."

She would lay money down that he never forgot a

thing, whether keyed in or not. She tamped down on her disappointment and gathered her courage.

"Boy, it's hot out here." She slid a hand under her hair and lifted it. Her back arched and her breasts pushed up and out, but he didn't spare her a glance. "Maybe I'll just cool off." She knelt near the water and splashed some onto her face, careful to let it drip down into her cleavage. "Uh-oh. I'm all wet now."

In more ways than one.

He still didn't look at her. "I've got an extra T-shirt under the seat on my bike if you need to dry off."

"Thanks, but I'm fine." She pushed to her feet and barely resisted kicking him in the side. That would get his attention.

And cause major damage. She wanted him in her bed, not the hospital. "It's a really nice night. Would you look at that moon?"

He didn't, and she re-evaluated her earlier decision. The toe of her shoe caught him in the ribs.

Hey, he was a vampire. He would heal.

"Ouch!" His head whipped around, and his ice-blue gaze stared up at her. "What the hell was that for?"

She shrugged. "Sorry." She gave him an innocent smile. "I guess I lost my balance."

He didn't look the least bit convinced, but at least he was looking at her.

Before she could reach for the strap of her tank top, however, he turned back to his PDA.

"My front drive shaft was a little shaky," he commented, as if trying to get his thoughts back on business. "I'll have to make some tweaks to it."

"This place is really great," she tried for more conversation. "Do you come here often?"

"I live here."

She glanced toward the opposite bank and the lush green grass that stretched toward a distant wall of trees. "Unless you're pitching a tent over there every night—one with Kryptonite walls—I doubt you live here."

A grin tugged at his mouth. "Kryptonite's for superheroes, sugar, not vampires, and I didn't mean here at the river. I meant here on the property." He motioned to the north. "I've got a place just beyond those trees over there."

"Oh." She remembered the name of the river and a light bulb went off in her brain. "Black Bottom as in Sam Black." The man he'd once been.

The man she'd betrayed.

"I…" she started, only to clamp down on her bottom lip. She couldn't change the past with a simple I'm sorry, no matter how heartfelt. And she certainly couldn't erase the hurt.

The only way to ease that would be to give him back the humanity that she took from him, which she fully intended to do.

Soon.

The hair on the back of her neck prickled, and once again she felt the strange awareness. They were catching up to her.

"So, um, do you come here often?" It sounded

cheesy even to her ears, but it was the only thing she could think of to say.

She needed to talk. To cut the tension that stretched so tightly between them.

"Every now and then. It's peaceful here. And wide open." He spared a glance at his surroundings. "It helps me think."

Because he couldn't think when he was cooped up and barricaded in during the day. Hiding from the sunlight. Smothering because of what he was.

"I know the feeling," she blurted before she could think better of it. "My folks had this old farmhouse, and I used to hide under the boards when I was first turned. I hated it. It was so dark. So damp. But at least it was safe."

"What about your folks?" He spared her a glance then, his gaze drilling into her for a long, piercing moment. "Did they really die in a fire? Or did you lie about that, too?"

She ignored the urge to turn, to run the way she'd been doing her entire life. But she couldn't escape her past. She knew that now. What's more, she didn't want to. Instinctively, her hand went to her throat, her fingers searching for the St. Benedict medal. Bare skin met bare skin, and she remembered that she'd left it back in her suitcase.

She stiffened and gathered her courage. "My mother did die in a fire." She hadn't deceived him about that. Not completely. "But my father…" She caught her lip for a long moment before the words trembled out. "My father is the one who turned me." She'd never actually said the words out loud to anyone. She'd never been able to.

Until now.

Suddenly, she couldn't seem to stop herself. Even more, she didn't want to.

She wanted to tell him the truth. And she did.

14

"HE WENT OUT gambling one night and didn't come home for three days." Her voice broke the calm silence. "That was typical for him, though. He was always leaving us, disappearing for days." She stared out over the water, seeing the old farmhouse instead.

Her father stood on the front porch. He wore his usual stained overalls, his shirt sleeves rolled up to reveal meaty forearms. The stench of moonshine rolled off him, along with something else.

A dark, forbidden anger that never failed to send her running into the fields to hide from him.

Her palms started to sweat, and she clutched at the medal that dangled around her neck. It matched the one that her mother wore. St. Benedict. The protector. The medal felt cold against her palm, and anxiety rolled through her. Along with fear.

Run. Hide.

She'd done just that so many times.

Often he'd found her, but sometimes—those blessed few times—he hadn't.

Run. Hide.

She hadn't had a chance to do either that night.

"I thought he was just drunk at first," she said, her lips trembling around the words. "He had that crazy look in his eyes the way he always did. But there was something else…I didn't know what it was at first. But then he opened his mouth, and I saw his fangs." She blinked against the sudden burning at the backs of her eyes.

"He attacked my mother before I could blink," she went on when she managed to find her voice. "One minute she was standing there, and the next her throat was ripped open and she was bleeding out onto the floor." He'd snatched the medal off the older woman's neck and lapped up the blood while Viv had watched. Terror pumping through her small body. Her own medal digging into her small hands. "He turned on me then. I tried to get away." A lump pushed its way into her throat, and she swallowed it back down. "I ran for the door, but he caught me. I fought him and knocked over one of the lanterns." She shook her head. "One minute my mother was just lying there, and the next her dress was on fire. I tried to help, but then he grabbed me and…" The words stumbled into one another, and she swallowed again.

The past was there, right in front of her. She could see the bright orange flames, feel the heat and the pain and the terror.

"That explains why you looked so freaked out at the fire back at the machine shop." His deep voice slid into her ears and drew her away from the carnage, back to the present.

The images faded, and she found herself staring at a lush stretch of green grass that led to a thick patch of trees.

She nodded. "By the time he was finished drinking from me, I was almost dead, and my mother had burned beyond recognition. It was too late for him to turn her. I wanted him to let me die, too, but he didn't. He wouldn't."

Because he was a cruel bastard who'd done nothing but hurt her since the day she'd been born. As a vampire, that cruelty had been magnified.

"He turned me and then he disappeared. I haven't seen him since." She faced Garret then, her gaze finally meeting his. "He didn't die like I told you, but I wished he had. He was a hateful man. He hit my mother and he…" She caught her bottom lip, fighting back the darker images—the ones she'd buried deep down inside—that threatened to swamp her. "He wasn't much better to me."

Garret's gaze brightened into a vicious red, and she knew he was pissed.

At her? Because she'd lied to him?

Or for her?

If she hadn't known better, she would have put her money on number two. But she'd hurt him too badly for him to care one way or the other.

She shrugged. "I've had a long time to come to terms with what happened to me, and I'm okay with it. But still, he should have died in that fire. In my mind, he did."

The red faded into an icy blue, and she was left to wonder if she'd only imagined his rage. "My dad eventually died of a heart attack," he told her, as if one admission deserved another. It didn't, but oddly enough, hearing his voice soothed the frantic beat of her heart and calmed the images that pushed and pulled inside of her. "My mom died of consumption. Not that I was there. I didn't trust myself to see them after I turned, so I took off."

"How did you find out what happened to them?" She shifted her attention away from her own demons, and concentrated on his.

He held up the PDA. "Technology is a beautiful thing." He grinned, easing the dark mood that had gripped them. His expression faded. "I'm really sorry about your mother."

He looked as surprised by the sincerity of his words as she was. But then the look vanished as he shifted his attention back to his PDA. "I really need to finish a few notes."

She stood there beside him for the next few moments trying to ignore the past that fluttered in and out of her head. Not the bad memories. No, those had faded along with the conversation. The memories that haunted her now featured the two of them. Outside. In the moonlight.

Talking. Sharing. Making love.

Not. Making love required being in love, which they weren't. No matter how much she'd pretended otherwise back then.

Rather, they'd had sex. Lots and lots and lots of sex.

Her body stirred, still fired up after her frenzied state

just moments ago. Hunger clawed inside of her. She felt itchy and tight. Anxious. Alive. And painfully aware of the vampire who sat so close.

Physically, that is.

Emotionally, he seemed a thousand miles away.

"I—I really ought to take some pictures of this for my article." With the information she already had from Eldin and several other businesses around town, she'd written the copy on Skull Creek, calling it the "sexiest small town in Texas." She'd e-mailed it to her editor tonight. All she needed now were a few more photos to support the text, and she would be finished.

The river and the moonlight definitely portrayed the sexy image she was trying to project to her readers. Besides, a few pictures would give her something to do while he finished with his notes. Then he would look at her long enough for her to seduce him.

She meant to walk to the pink chopper and retrieve the camera she'd stowed under the seat. She really did. But her feet seemed to have a will all their own. Instead of turning, she stepped forward, out onto the water. Her feet barely skimmed the surface—another vamp perk—as she made her way around in front of him.

He didn't glance up from his PDA.

Doubt pushed past the determination dictating her actions, and she almost turned and headed back to the riverbank. She should wait.

She would wait.

If she had the time.

But the minutes were slipping away, and Molly and

Cruz were getting closer. The phone call was evidence. Enough to prompt her to finish the article and tie up that loose end. The prickling awareness that followed her around, reminding her of Washington and the ambush, was even more proof.

It was now or never.

She backed up several feet, putting a little distance between them while she worked up her nerve. Finally, she stopped.

Her ears tuned to the music, and she closed her eyes for a long moment to block out the man hunkered down on the riverbank. The beat filled her head and thrummed through her body as she started to move.

She swayed, a subtle rotation of her hips from side to side. A vision slid into her head, and the past pulled her back. To the small barn where she'd found him saddling up to ride out and join his regiment.

One look into her eyes, and he'd forgotten all about the horse. He'd stripped them both down to nothing and pressed her down into the soft, sweet-smelling hay one last time.

He spread her legs wide and plunged deep inside. Her eyes closed as pleasure swelled and crashed over her. Her nerve endings came alive. Her heart thundered. Her ears rang. Her blood pounded.

She wasn't sure how she heard his voice, but she did. The deep timbre pushed its way past her thundering heart and sizzled along her nerve endings.

"Look at me, Viv."

The memory faded as she opened her eyes to find

Garret—a very real Garret—staring back at her, and she realized that the voice hadn't been her memory this time.

She had his full attention now.

He'd pushed to his feet, the PDA forgotten in his hand as he stared across the mirrorlike surface at her. His ice-blue eyes gleamed in the moonlit darkness. Tension held his body tight. His muscles bunched beneath his T-shirt. Taut lines carved his face, making him seem harsh, fierce, predatory.

He was every bit the vampire she'd made him.

At the same time, there was something familiar in his eyes.

Passion.

Lust.

Love.

She ditched the last thought. He'd never loved her. Not then, and certainly not now.

But want…

He definitely wanted her.

Enough to forgive the past, forget the hurt and betrayal, and take the initiative?

There was only one way to find out.

WHAT IN THE HELL was she doing?

Garret watched as she started to move to the slow, sexy song that poured from the radio. Her hips shifted from side to side in a seductive way that made his muscles bunch and his groin tighten.

She slid her hands beneath her hair and lifted the silky curtain before letting it fall back down around her shoulders. She wasn't as practiced as an actual stripper, but she was pretty damned good.

Enough that his dick throbbed and hardened and, just like that, he had a massive erection.

It's not her. It's you, buddy. It's who you are. What you are.

She arched her back, and her breasts jutted forward, her hard nipples perfectly outlined beneath her sparkly tank top. His mouth watered at the memory of the throbbing tips deep in his mouth, her skin slick and wet beneath his hands. His entire body shook with need.

Hunger sliced through him, and his groin tightened.

He tried to fight the primitive urges that gripped him, but instead found himself thinking that maybe, just maybe, having sex with her wouldn't be such a bad thing.

It wasn't like he was falling for her all over again.

He was stronger now. Immune to her vamp mojo because he had his own.

No, this wasn't about falling for her. It was about falling into bed with her. Or, in this case, smack dab onto the river bank.

A little body-slapping, and he would see that she was nothing special. That he'd simply been mesmerized all those years ago.

He wasn't mesmerized now.

He was hungry. Horny.

He needed to press himself between her legs and drive into her slick flesh over and over until she climaxed and he drank in her sweet energy.

Even more, he needed to shatter the illusion that had haunted him for the past two hundred years.

Viv Darland wasn't his one and only—she never had been—and having sex with her was a surefire way to prove she was no different from any other woman out there.

Then he could stop fantasizing. Dreaming. Remembering.

Once and for all.

_15_

SHE'D FINALLY GOTTEN his full, undivided attention. She just couldn't decide if that was a good thing or a bad thing.

His expression was unreadable, his eyes hard and unwavering, his mouth set in a grim line as if he fought some internal battle.

Viv trailed her tongue over her bottom lip, determined to do everything she could to tip the scales in her favor. She touched a finger to her throat. A few fluttering strokes against the steady beat of her pulse, and her own hunger stirred. Her ears prickled, sifting through the sensory overload—the buzz of crickets, the scurry of critters, the whistle of the breeze, the occasional whinny of a horse—until she heard only the thud of her own heart and the slow, intoxicating melody drifting from the speakers.

A deep voice on the radio crooned about making love all weekend, and she slid a finger to the edge of her tank top, tracing the line where flesh met soft cotton before moving to the strap. Hooking her finger beneath, she eased the material down over her shoulder. Lifting her opposite arm, she did the same with the other strap until the cotton sagged around her shoulders.

She gave her upper body a little shimmy. The tank top rode lower on her torso until the material caught on her bare, aroused nipples.

Garret swallowed, and the air grew hot and shimmery between them.

She could feel the heat rolling off his muscular body, see the frantic beat of his pulse at the base of his neck, smell the rich, musky aroma of hot, aroused male. She knew then that he wasn't half as indifferent as she'd first suspected.

A surge of feminine power went through her, and she pushed the straps of her shirt down until the material hugged her waist. Grasping the cotton, she eased it over her hips. She gave a little shake, and the top slid down her thighs, past her knees to puddle around her ankles. Leaning down, she caught the edge of the material and stepped free. Then with all the confidence of a sexy woman who'd been seducing men forever, she smiled. Just a faint crook to her lips that told him there would be more—much more—to come.

Cool night air slid over her bare arms and breasts, but it did little to ease her rising body temperature. His hot molten gaze fanned the flames, heating her body, her blood, until she felt the air sizzle around her.

She touched the undersides of her breasts, cupping the full mounds, weighing them and feeling the heat of her own fingertips against the soft flesh. All the while she imagined that it was Garret's touch that seared her.

She skimmed her palms over her nipples, and they throbbed in response. Her stomach quivered beneath her fluttering fingertips as she moved on. Down. Around her belly button. To the zipper of her skirt.

A few tugs, and the opening slid free, her zipper parted and the material sagged. She rocked her hips in time to the slow, sweet, twangy song that filled the night air, and the skirt slithered down her hips. Her legs. She toed the denim to the side with her high heel.

She wore a silky red thong that matched her high heels and made her feel just as decadent. She traced the very edge before trailing her fingertips over the satin V. Back and forth. Side to side. Desire speared her, so sharp and potent, that her vision clouded, and her nipples hardened and quivered. Her eyes closed, and her need magnified.

Anxiety rushed through her and made her entire body tremble, but she wasn't giving in to it.

Not just yet.

She gathered her control and focused on his burning gaze rather than the damnable hunger that pushed and pulled inside of her. With one fingertip, she teased the elastic at the edge of her undies before dipping a finger beneath. She touched the damp, swollen flesh between her legs, and her nerves hummed. Another lingering stroke, and she pushed deep inside her drenched flesh.

Pressure spiked through her, and she gasped.

She'd touched herself many times in this exact same way during more than one fantasy starring the hot, hunky vampire standing in front of her. But it had never felt the way it did now.

So real.

So intense.

So…pleasurable.

Another move of her fingers, and her body swayed from the sensation rippling along her nerve endings. But it wasn't enough to satisfy the restless need inside of her. Not even close.

She didn't want her own touch. She wanted his.

Sliding her finger free of her panties, she hooked the edge and slid the material down her legs. Stepping free, she faced him, her skin bathed in moonlight, her nipples hard and inviting, her body wet and ready.

He just stood there.

Watching.

Waiting.

"I came here for this," she heard herself say. Her gaze locked with his. "For you."

She wasn't sure why she told him the truth. Except that she'd already put herself out there by stripping naked, so there seemed no point in denying it anymore. That, and she wanted him to know that he wasn't just any man to her.

Not then and not now.

He didn't move for a long moment, as if letting her words sink in. Disbelief flashed in his gaze, followed by a strange glimmer that burned up any and everything else. He dropped his PDA to the riverbank and reached for the hem of his T-shirt. Pulling the soft cotton over his head, he tossed it to the side.

He was every bit as rough and rugged as she remembered.

Muscles carved his torso, from his bulging biceps and shoulders to the rippled plane of his abdomen. Dark, silky hair sprinkled his chest and narrowed to a tiny funnel of silk that disappeared beneath the button fly of his faded jeans.

Her gaze swept down to the prominent bulge beneath his zipper, and her pulse quickened.

His boots barely made a ripple as he strode across the water and ate up the distance that separated them. He stopped just inches shy.

Close, but not close enough.

"I'm not the man you remember." She wasn't sure if it was an admission or a warning.

Her doubts stirred and suddenly, she couldn't help but wonder if maybe, just maybe, she'd come to Skull Creek for nothing.

He was different now.

And there was a very real possibility that her reaction to him would be different, as well.

Maybe sex with him would be as uneventful as it had been with every other male in her past.

Maybe.

Probably.

"I'm not a man at all," he added.

She clung to a small ripple of hope and fingered her sensitive nipple. "Neither am I."

A grin tugged at his lips, followed by a fierce, hungry look as he watched her play with herself. She plucked the ripe tip, rubbed and stirred until a gasp worked its way up her throat.

"I've pictured you like this, you know." He reached out to replace her hand with his own. The rough pad of his thumb flicked her, and the tip hardened even more. Her areola tightened and puckered. A growl vibrated up his throat. "Standing in the moonlight with your eyes bright and your body trembling." His gaze flashed and his mouth opened just enough for her to see the gleaming white tips of his fangs. "In my dreams. My fantasies."

Excitement stirred deep inside of her, along with her own hunger. Her gut clenched, and her legs quivered. "I've fantasized about you, too." She wasn't sure why she told him, except he spoke so freely and suddenly she wanted to, as well.

She wanted to talk to him the way she had back then. And she wanted him to listen.

To care.

The notion struck, and she stiffened. Caring? This wasn't about caring. It was about passion. Fast, furious, blazing passion.

He thumbed her nipple again before dipping his head. His tongue flicked out, and he licked her. Once, twice.

Slowly. Meticulously.

Because he wasn't turned on enough. Not yet.

Dangling, she could almost hear Winona say.

"Geez, it's getting hot," she commented as he slid his hands under her breasts.

"Not nearly hot enough." He kneaded the soft, round globes.

Excitement flared in the pit of her stomach, and she closed her eyes for a long, nerve-wracking moment. She couldn't… She wouldn't…

She opened her eyes and stared at her feet, focusing on the quickest means of escape from the delicious sensation wreaking havoc on her control.

"I—I think maybe it's time to cool off." She willed herself to drop, plunging straight down into the water and out of his grasp.

The cool liquid closed over her head, and she relished the sudden change of temperature. She needed to calm down, to douse the inferno that raged deep inside and threatened to seize control.

She wasn't taking the lead and killing her chances for a bona fide orgasm.

She wasn't.

She stayed under for several long moments, until her heart calmed enough for her to actually think again.

Finally, she moved her arms and legs, swimming back toward the shimmering moonlight overhead. She broke the surface with a soft plunk and opened her eyes to find him nowhere in sight.

She wiped a hand over her face. Other than the two motorcycles, the bank sat empty, the trees shrouding everything else in darkness.

Surely, he wouldn't leave his motorcycle?

Then again, if he'd changed his mind…

Instead of upping the challenge, maybe her retreat had given him time to come to his senses.

To run.

The truth echoed in her head as she did a complete three-sixty in the water, her gaze searching every inch of the surrounding bank. A faint rustle thundered through her head, and her gaze snapped to the stretch of lush vegetation to her right. A rabbit darted across the ground before disappearing into the trees. A cricket buzzed, hopping from one distant branch to the other. A firefly sparked, bobbing through the trees.

She glanced down at the water, her gaze pushing into the dark depths, but she saw only the steady kick of her own legs, the flap of her arms. On the surface, her reflection stared back at her.

Her hair was plastered to her head. Water dripped from the tip of her nose. Black circles rimmed her eyes and made streaks down her cheeks—

What the hell?

She peered closer, and a sinking feeling gripped the pit of her stomach. She hadn't used waterproof mascara. She hadn't even thought about it.

But then, she hadn't had a clue she'd be going for a swim. No, she'd pictured herself having sex tonight, not playing cat and mouse in the river.

She wiped frantically at her face, but that only smeared the black even more. She'd just splashed a handful of water onto her face to try to wash some of it off when she felt the soft brush against the inside of one ankle.

She jumped, kicking her legs and flailing around. While she might be up to a game with Garret, she wasn't going one on one with a fish. Or a snake.

Not that she was vulnerable to snakes. It was just the

thought of something she couldn't see slithering around her ankles that sent goose bumps dancing up and down her arms. She definitely didn't do snakes.

Just as the notion struck, something brushed her other ankle, and she kicked out.

To hell with this.

She focused, gathering her strength and energy, and started to lift herself out of the water. But then the faint brush turned to a steel-like grip as fingers wrapped around her ankle and jerked her back down.

The water closed over her and she went completely under. Deeper and deeper. She flailed, fighting for a split-second until she felt the strong arms close around her, and she knew it wasn't a snake.

Her eyes opened and through the shimmering water, she saw Garret, his face only inches from her. His eyes blazed with a hunger so bright and intense that she felt like she'd go up in flames.

She had the sudden thought that she should definitely give Winona a great, big fat bonus for her advice, but then his lips touched hers, and she stopped thinking altogether.

Shazam!

16

HE'D FANTASIZED ABOUT kissing her so many times over the years. But nothing, not even the most decadent dream, prepared him for the real thing.

Her lips were soft and full beneath his plundering mouth and an electrical current ran from his lips, straight to his growing erection. He pushed his tongue deep, stroking and delving. He was through denying himself. He meant to sample every inch of her, savor her essence on his lips, make her writhe and moan until she knew without a doubt that he was her equal—a seductive, mesmerizing vampire with pure sex on his mind.

He pulled her flush against his body as they hung suspended in the sparkling depths of the water. He let his hands roam over her naked body and marveled at the feel. She was softer than he remembered. More voluptuous.

Impossible, he knew.

She was a vampire. The same yesterday, today, tomorrow. He knew that, yet he found himself slowing down and re-learning every inch of her anyway.

The dip at the base of her spine, the soft hollow just beneath her rib cage, the roundness of her ass, the smooth, sensitive inside of each thigh.

He drew her closer, pulling her legs around him and locking her ankles at the small of his back. Then he settled her firmly against the rock-hard length barely contained by his zipper.

She wrapped her arms around his neck and hung on as he rocked her. The coarse material of his jeans rasped against her clitoris, and he felt her tremble.

The water stirred around them, bubbling from the heat rolling off their bodies. At the rate they were going, it wouldn't be long until the entire river started to steam.

He focused his thoughts and willed them to move toward the surface and higher…until they cleared the river completely and levitated a few feet above. Water dripped off of them, sprinkling down as he moved them toward the opposite river bank and the soft patch of thick grass.

When his bare feet touched the lush growth, he kissed her again, exploring and tasting for the next few frantic moments before he loosened his grip. Easing her to the ground, he slid her down his hard length, letting her feel every inch of how badly he wanted her.

A gasp parted her lips. He caught the sound as he kissed her again, hard and insistent. His hands were everywhere, touching, branding, reminding her of the past and how much he'd changed.

That was the goal here. To prove that he wasn't the same man any more than she was the same woman.

He'd been as charged up sexually, of course, but he'd had a far different goal in mind.

Back then, he'd been concerned with both giving and receiving pleasure. But now... Now it wasn't about having his own orgasm. It was about sustaining himself, growing stronger, feeding.

It was about giving her an orgasm and soaking up the energy he so desperately needed.

Ditto for her. Or so he thought. But she made no move to turn him on and push him toward the edge. Rather, she seemed content to be on the receiving end. As if her goal had nothing to do with the beast that lived and breathed inside of her and everything to do with the woman who stood before him.

As if.

He had to give her credit. She was one hell of an actress. Then and now.

Desperate sounds worked their way past her luscious lips as he touched her. Her breasts plumped beneath his fingertips. Her nipples hardened.

He moved lower, stroking the heat between her legs, plunging, mimicking what he was going to do to her. He slipped his hands between her legs to find her warm and slick and oh, so ready.

She managed to tear her lips away. "No," she gasped the minute his fingertip pushed a delicious inch into her steamy heat. "Not like this...I..." She licked her lips, her eyes bright with desire. "I—I want you inside of me."

He wanted it, too.

He wanted to bury himself deep and forget the rest of the world and explode.

A realization that made him all the more determined to hold back.

The way he would with any woman.

That's all she was to him.

Any woman.

Every woman.

He ignored the last thought and slid a finger deep inside of her. She moaned, the sound vibrating up her throat, feeding the excitement that coiled inside of him.

"No," she said again when he plunged a second finger inside, but the word was softer, weaker.

He withdrew and pushed back in. Her muscles quivered around him, and a drop of wetness slid across his palm. Her lips trembled as he took her mouth in another kiss. Deeper than the last. Hotter. Wetter.

He pleasured her with his hand and his mouth for the next several moments until she clung to him. A soft cry bubbled from her lips. A tremor went through her, and energy rushed into him from every point of contact.

He fixated on the empowering buzz and let it feed his strength. His senses sharpened and magnified and the fog in his head seemed to clear.

But it wasn't enough, he realized when her climax subsided and the buzz faded to a distant hum. The beast stirred, restless and demanding and not the least bit satisfied, and a growl worked its way up his throat.

The deep rumbling pushed past the ringing in Viv's

ears and drew her gaze to his. She pulled away to stare up at him.

His eyes fired with a predatory light. A hiss slid past his lips and he opened his mouth. His fangs flashed, gleaming in the moonlight, and a crazy excitement welled inside of her.

Crazy because she couldn't let him actually bite her. She wouldn't. If he drank from her, or vice versa, it would forge a nearly unbreakable bond between them. They would be one.

He would know her darkest fears and her deepest secrets.

He would know the truth.

She stumbled back, but he refused to let her retreat. He matched her step for step until she came up against one of the massive trees that circled the clearing.

Gone was the passionate man who'd pleasured her for hours on end. Instead, he'd turned into a raw primitive savage.

A vampire.

The truth stirred a wave of guilt, but then he reached for her.

One hand dove into the hair at the base of her skull while the other pressed into the small of her back. He tugged her head back until her neck was fully exposed. The sharp edge of his fangs grazed the tender flesh, rasping and prickling just enough to draw one sweet drop.

She hissed, warning him away, but he wasn't about to be put off.

He followed the crimson trail with his seductive

mouth and licked his way over her clavicle, down the slope of her breast until it reached her nipple.

He sucked her into his mouth, and a burst of pleasure sliced through her from her head clear to her toes.

But while he rasped her with his fangs, he didn't sink them deep. She realized then that he didn't want the bond between them any more than she did.

Relief swept through her, followed by a surge of disappointment.

He didn't give her a chance to analyze the strange reaction. He urged her down to the soft grass and straddled her.

The faded material of his wet jeans hugged his hard thighs, showing every ripple of muscle. His bare torso gleamed with a fine sheen of water that caught flickers of moonlight.

She reached up and trailed her hands along his slick muscled flesh. His shoulders rippled and bulged beneath her palms. She splayed her fingers in the hair covering his chest, her touch tentative, restrained as she followed the whorl of silk as it narrowed and descended to his abdomen. She stopped just shy of the waistband to his jeans.

Her hunger raged, urging her on. She balled her fingers against the need. Her body stiffened. She forced her gaze away, up over his rock-hard abdomen, his broad chest, his corded neck, to his face.

His eyes burned, reflecting the pure, ravaging hunger that she felt inside.

"Please," she heard herself beg. Because she'd gone without the sweet, drenching heat for so long.

Without him.

As if he read her mind, he leaned down. His tongue flicked a ripe nipple, and she gasped. His mouth was hot and wet as he drew her in, tonguing and laving the stiff peak until she arched against him.

"Unzip me," he said when he finally drew away. He caught her hand and pressed it to his crotch.

Her fingers fluttered over the zipper, the metal hot beneath her touch. Because he was hot, his skin on fire. The air around them shimmered, and she could practically see the sparks in the translucent depths of his eyes.

"I can't..." Because if she reached out this time, she wouldn't be able to stop. She would unzip him, roll him over and straddle him, and that would be the kiss of death. He had to be the leader.

"You can," he said. "And you will." He leaned down and flicked her nipple again, teasing and torturing even longer this time until she couldn't not touch him.

The zipper hissed, and he sprang hot and eager into her hands. Her attention riveted on his heated, pulsing flesh. He was as smooth as satin and rock-hard.

She trailed her fingers over him, touching the ripe head of his desire. He jumped in her hands, and she barely resisted the urge to dip her head, to taste him.

Instead, she wrapped her arms around his neck and pulled him down for a kiss that surprised them both. It was a bold move, but not half as aggressive as what she wanted to do to him.

Her passion seemed to feed his, and soon he was back in the driver's seat. He kissed her harder, faster, deeper. He pulled away long enough to peel off the wet jeans and then he joined her on the soft grass.

He parted her legs and settled himself between them. He rasped his erection up and down her slick folds before entering her in one powerful surge.

The sudden sense of fullness deep inside sent shockwaves pulsing through her body. Her inner muscles contracted, sucking him in. Pressure erupted in her belly.

He started to move, plunging and withdrawing, over and over, and the pressure mounted. His movements picked up and he pumped harder, faster, pushing her closer to the edge just the way he had so many times in the past.

But the heat felt sweeter this time, sharper, more intense than anything in her memory.

The pinnacle was steeper this time, the crest higher. When she finally reached the top and plunged over the edge into orgasmic bliss, it was much more powerful than anything she remembered.

Sensation crashed over her and sucked her under for several long moments. Her heart pounded, and her blood rushed. Her body clenched around his and held on. Pleasure drenched her, all-consuming for the next few moments as her heart stopped and her body clenched.

She stared up at him, into him, waiting for the rush of warmth as he followed her over the edge.

But instead of pushing even deeper and letting

himself go, he pulled out a few inches until only the very tip of his erection stayed inside. His muscles bunched as he held himself back and loomed over her. His eyes grew even brighter and a growl rumbled from deep in his chest. He trembled as he drank in the sweet sexual energy of her climax.

She felt the draw where the very tip of his penis nestled inside her slick folds. The tremble of flesh against flesh turned her on as much as the actual sex. Her nipples throbbed, and her clit started to quiver again. Her body vibrated, and sensation rushed through her.

And then all of a sudden it was happening again. Pleasure crashed over her. She cried out, closing her eyes and arching against him for several long moments.

Until her body calmed enough for her to open her eyes.

She found him still poised above her, his body tense, his teeth clamped together as if he'd been waiting on her to look up before he let himself go.

Sheer longing flashed in his gaze. Or so she thought. But then he blinked, and the emotion faded into the icy blue depths of his eyes and he did the last thing she expected.

He pulled away.

"We should be getting back." His voice was gruff as he turned away from her, his erection still rock-hard. He reached for his jeans. "I've got a lot of work to do."

"I. . ." She caught her bottom lip to stop its sudden trembling as she pushed herself into a sitting position and tried to calm the shock beating at her temples. "I— I need to get back to work myself."

Silence stretched around them as he stepped into his jeans and pulled them on. A hiss vibrated up his throat as he tugged the zipper over his erection. She almost reached out for him. A few strokes of her hand, the warm heat of her mouth, and she could give him the release he so desperately needed.

Then again, maybe he didn't need her. Maybe he wasn't aching or hurting.

Maybe he was more than satisfied from her climax alone.

The possibility haunted her as he helped her to her feet. There were no lingering touches. Rather, he dropped her hand as quickly as possible. In the blink of an eye, he stood on the opposite river bank where the motorcycles sat.

By the time she joined him, he'd retrieved the spare shirt he'd mentioned earlier from beneath his seat. He tossed it to her before turning to pick up his own T-shirt that still lay where he'd left it.

Her gaze went to the water. She'd done her striptease on the river, which meant that her own clothes were several feet under by now. She debated a quick dive to see if she could find at least her undies, but Garret straddled his motorcycle and gunned the engine and she knew she didn't have time.

Not if she was going to follow him back.

She slipped the giant T-shirt over her head. The cotton dropped to mid-thigh which afforded her enough modesty to climb onto her own motorcycle.

"Let's go." He didn't wait for a reply. He gunned the

engine, shifted into gear and took off as if the Devil himself were in hot pursuit.

Viv blinked back the sudden stinging behind her eyes, gunned the engine and followed.

You did it, she reminded herself as she trailed behind.

Sex.

Orgasm.

Shazam!

Oddly enough, she didn't feel any more satisfied than when they'd first ridden out to the river.

It was the bike, of course.

She wasn't wearing undies, and the steady pulse of the engine was getting to her.

No way was she feeling so out of sorts because Garret hadn't had his own orgasm. So what if he'd held himself back, content just to drink up her energy?

He was a vampire, and that's what vampires did. Sure, he never would have done such a thing if he'd been human, but he wasn't. And what difference did it make anyway?

She hadn't come to Skull Creek to give him an orgasm. She'd come in pursuit of her own.

Which meant that what he had or hadn't felt didn't concern her. She'd accomplished her goal, end of story.

That's what she told herself. But she couldn't shake the hollowness in the pit of her stomach or the ache in her chest. Feelings that magnified when she followed him into the back parking lot of Skull Creek Choppers.

He was already climbing off his chopper when she killed the engine. "You can leave the keys in the ignition.

I'll grab them later." And then he turned and walked away from her without so much as a "See ya."

Viv watched him disappear through the back door before she climbed off the chopper and headed for her car. A lump worked its way up her throat as she climbed behind the wheel and headed back to the motel.

She swallowed and blinked frantically a few times. She wasn't going to cry. She should be happy. She was happy.

She'd done it. She'd had an honest-to-God orgasm.

And just in the nick of time, she realized when she reached her motel room.

The thought struck the moment she unlocked the door and stared into the pitch-black interior. She stalled in the doorway. Awareness crawled down her spine and her survival instincts fired to life.

Turn. Fight. Run.

No more.

She closed her eyes as the shadows closed in and a hand clamped around her throat.

It was finally time to set things right.

17

IN THE BLINK of an eye, she found herself whirled around and shoved up against the nearest wall by a hard male body. Bright green eyes stared down at her, and her memory stirred.

"Sheriff Keller?" Her gaze sliced through the darkness and drank in the familiar face of Matt Keller, the sheriff who'd threatened her with trespassing and escorted her off the mountain in Washington.

"No, it's the Easter Bunny."

It was him, all right.

He stood well over six feet with dark black hair cut short and neat. A day's growth of stubble shadowed his angular jaw. A scar zig-zagged its way from his temple down his right cheek. He wasn't the most handsome man, but he had a rough edge about him that no doubt attracted more than his share of women.

She wasn't one of them, of course. Despite the hunger that lived and breathed inside of her, she hadn't been the least bit attracted when she'd first met him.

She'd been too preoccupied with her story, too worked up over the strange prickling awareness that Cruz and Molly were catching up to her.

"You went back to the crime scene," he told her, "I know because we found a strange DNA on the front porch." His gaze hardened. "You compromised the evidence."

"I didn't mean to. I—I went back to get a few pictures and I cut myself."

"There was an awful lot of blood for a minor cut."

"I'm a heavy bleeder."

He didn't look as if he bought the explanation, but he let go of her anyway. But not before his gaze brightened to a brilliant, glowing green, and she started to wonder if there was more than rugged good looks feeding Matt Keller's success with the ladies.

Especially when she stared deep into his eyes and saw…nothing. No hang-ups. No family history. No work-related goals or plans for the future. Just a blank wall.

A vampire?

Nah. She would have sensed as much. As it was, she felt only a humming awareness, as if Molly and Cruz were close. But not too close.

Not yet.

She stared into Matt's eyes, searching for some clue that he was anything other than a human who'd managed to shield his thoughts. Some could, particularly if they knew there were vampires out there trying to crawl into their heads. She focused all of her attention, determined to crack the wall and see the truth.

As if he knew what she was up to, he turned away,

averting those glowing green eyes as he flipped on a nearby light.

"There," he said. "That's better." He closed the motel room door. "Now we can talk."

"About?"

"The Butcher. You went back to the scene of the crime. You took pictures. You gathered evidence. I want it."

"But I didn't. I meant to, but then I—" she swallowed "—cut myself and I had to leave to find a first aid kit."

He didn't buy it, but he didn't call her out, either. "Still, you've been following the case from day one. The West Hollywood murder. The Portland couple. You've taken pictures and asked questions and I figure you know a helluva lot more than you realize."

"So you came all the way to Texas to pick my brain?"

"I'm this close to cracking the case—and that's the problem. I'm too close to the killer." He shook his head. "I thought if we compared notes, it might help me figure out what I'm missing. This guy claims he's a celebrity, and you know celebrities."

Which is why she'd gotten involved in the first place. Gossip rags didn't cover grisly murders unless there was the possibility of something really sensational. Like Brad Pitt or Tom Hanks or some other A-list actor being possessed by the ghost of Ted Bundy.

It wasn't all that likely, but then neither was the three-headed alien baby born in Oregon.

"I seriously doubt my notes could help you very much."

"I'll be the judge of that once you hand them over."

"I'd be happy to, but I gave everything to my editor at the magazine." Along with her resignation. She scribbled down a phone number. "Call and ask for Louise. Tell her I gave you the number. I'm sure she can e-mail you a copy of my notes."

He nodded. "I talked to her when I started looking for you." He must have noticed her curious expression because he added, "I followed your paper trail. You used your Visa to buy the airline ticket from L.A. to San Antonio. From there, I followed you to a gas station about twenty miles up on the interstate. I made a few phone calls to the surrounding towns until I hit pay dirt here. Some clerk answered at the motel, and when I mentioned your name, he seemed nervous. Now I know why."

"You couldn't have just tracked down my cell phone number and called me up?"

He shrugged. "I didn't think about it."

Yeah, right. A phone number was more than a logical answer if all he'd wanted was to ask her a few questions. Unless he hadn't been half as anxious to talk to her as he was to find out her whereabouts.

To find her.

Unconsciously, her hand went to her throat, her fingers searching for the comforting warmth of her St. Benedict medal before she remembered that she'd stashed it in her suitcase.

"Sorry about the choke hold," he said, noticing the path of her hand. "You broke the law once, and I wasn't one hundred percent sure you wouldn't add assaulting a police officer to your rap sheet."

"I doubt I could take you."

He didn't look as if he believed the statement anymore than she did. As if he knew she wasn't the mild-mannered reporter she pretended to be.

"I seriously doubt you'll find any solid leads in my notes," she blurted, eager to ignore the strange thought. He wasn't a vampire, which meant he couldn't know the truth about her.

"I'll be the judge of that." He stashed the slip of paper with the contact information in his shirt pocket. "I'm staying just down the hall. I'll give your editor a call first thing in the morning. You'll be around tomorrow, right? In case I need clarification on anything?" She nodded, and he stared at her again, his gaze glowing, searching. "We'll talk once I figure things out," he finally said.

"I hope you find what you're looking for," she called out to his retreating back.

"I already did," he said and then he disappeared.

What was that supposed to mean?

The question haunted her as she stared at the closed door. He'd gone to a lot of trouble to find her just to get his hands on her notes.

Unless the notes were just a cover, and he wasn't half as interested in her research as he was in her.

"I already did."

His words echoed in her head, and his image flashed in her mind—his knowing expression, his odd gaze.

She'd noticed his eyes back in Washington when he'd escorted her off the mountain. But then she'd been ambushed by Cruz and Molly. She'd forgotten all about Keller, about the strange glow of his eyes and the fact that no matter how hard she'd tried, she hadn't been able to read his thoughts.

She'd forgotten about everything except surviving.

The notion stirred her suspicion.

Sheriff Matt Keller had shown up just minutes before Molly and Cruz back in Washington. Had he led them to her?

Was he leading them to her now?

The question stalled in her head and sent a burst of fear through her. She threw the lock on the door and peered past the edge of the curtains.

The shadowy walkway remained empty. In the distance, she could see a light on in the lobby. Eldin sat behind the registration desk, his gaze hooked on a nearby television, his hands busy with a platter of nachos.

Relief swept through. A crazy feeling because she'd already accepted her fate. The possibility that Sheriff Keller might be speeding up her fate by leading Molly and Cruz to her shouldn't have freaked her out.

It did.

Not because she was afraid to die, but because she was afraid to die without knowing the truth about her feelings for Garret.

The truth crystallized as she stood there in the window, her hand gripping the drape, her body still throbbing from their earlier encounter.

She wanted to right off the pounding of her heart and the trembling of her hands as fear. Because there was a very real possibility that Keller was linked to Cruz and Molly. But she knew it was more.

It was Garret.

Because she loved him?

She'd never thought so. Sure, she'd pretended that what she'd felt had been the real thing back then, but she'd never known. How could she? Her parents' relationship had been one of fear and dominance. There'd been no kind words, no soft feelings. She'd never seen love firsthand, and she'd never, ever felt it. While her mother had, indeed, cared for her, she'd been too busy worrying over her own survival to have anything left over for her daughter. And her father... He'd shown her only cruelty and hatred. Likewise, her existence had been a string of meaningless encounters, all fueled by hunger.

And so she'd written off the tingling in her stomach, the trembling in her knees and the strange warmth in her chest as pure, uncomplicated lust.

Physical rather than emotional.

She'd convinced herself that the only reason she'd reacted to him so intensely way back when was because he'd taken the lead and swept her off her feet. He'd treated her like a woman and so she'd reacted like one.

But if she gave in to the hungry beast inside of her and swept him off his feet, she wouldn't come anywhere close to having an orgasm.

Right?

Maybe.

Probably.

Still, she couldn't help but wonder as she stepped into the shower, if maybe there was more to it.

If he was more.

Maybe she reacted to him not because he was the only man who'd ever taken the lead, but because he was the only man, period.

Her one true love.

It shouldn't have mattered. Regardless, it wouldn't change her fate. If anything, it would make her all the more determined to set things right. She knew that, but she still couldn't close her eyes and push him out of her head when she finally toweled off and crawled into bed.

Instead, she tossed and turned and ended up staring at the ceiling.

She'd spent far too long—almost two centuries to be exact—wondering what it would feel like to love and be loved. While she had no illusions that Garret felt anything that strong for her——he'd been far too controlled tonight—she knew there was a real possibility that she loved him.

She climbed from the bed and reached for her clothes. While she had no clue if what she felt even came close to the real thing, she wasn't going to pass up the chance to find out.

To feel it. To really and truly feel it.

If only for a little while.

18

"THE MAN'S REAL NAME is John Darrington. It's probably an alias like the other, but there's no way to know for sure without checking further. His last known address is in Chicago," Dalton MacGregor's voice carried over the cell phone the minute Garret picked up. "I'm e-mailing it to you right now, along with my notes."

Garret paused, pitch fork in one hand, his cell phone clenched tight in the other. "You're sure it's him?"

"Based on the information that you gave me, this is the man you're looking for. He had actual contact with the blogger who gave the description of him. Based on everyone I've talked to, it's him, right down to the medallion that you described."

Garret could still feel the cold metal dangling over him, brushing his skin as the figure loomed over him.

"Do you want me to fly to Chicago and check it out myself?"

"You've done enough. I'll take it from here. Send me everything, and I'll leave first thing in the morning." Garret hung up and dialed Jake.

"We've got him," he told his friend.

"Really?" Excitement fueled the one word. "You're not shitting me, are you?"

"I'm flying out at sundown tomorrow to check it out. Twenty-four hours from now, you just might be getting ready to watch the sun rise."

"I'll go with you."

"No. You stay with Nikki and the others. This is something I need to do by myself."

Garret needed to face his past, to finally see the man's face. He wanted the bits and pieces of what he remembered to finally fit together in a clear, solid picture.

And then he wanted to shatter that picture and destroy the man who'd destroyed him.

He did.

So why didn't he feel even a fifth the excitement he'd heard in Jake's voice?

Because killing the Ancient One wouldn't solve Garret's problem.

It wouldn't make Viv love him the way he loved her.

Wait a second. Love? She couldn't love him any more than he could love her.

Hell, he didn't love her.

Tonight had proved as much. He'd held tight to his control and resisted the urge to climax.

Barely.

The realization followed him around the barn as he pitched hay for the three mares he had stabled inside. They were about to foal and he wanted them comfortable.

The horses stirred, dancing around their stalls, completely alert to his presence and fearful of it.

For now.

But come tomorrow night things would be different. He could help foal the mares, and he could start taming Delilah. He would have his life back. His humanity.

If only he wanted it half as much as he wanted Viv.

The truth pushed and pulled and haunted him for the next half hour as he tried to work off the sexual energy stringing his body tight. He couldn't, regardless of how hard he pitched or how fast he moved.

He wanted her.

In a way he'd never wanted any woman before.

Because she meant more to him than an easy lay and a way to feed the beast inside of him.

Much, much more.

He didn't want to believe it, but then she appeared in the barn doorway, and the sight of her outlined in the moonlight stopped him cold.

There was nothing provocative about her faded pink sweats and worn tennis shoes, but his gut tightened anyway. Her eyes sparked a bright, brilliant blue, and the minute his gaze locked with hers, his heart stalled in his chest.

He loved her, all right, and that made him all the more determined to resist her when she stepped forward. He'd given her his heart once before. He wasn't about to make the same mistake twice.

No, he would play it cool. Controlled.

"What are you doing here?" he asked, trying to sound indifferent.

"I thought I'd see where you live." She glanced around. "It's nice."

"It's a barn."

"Yeah, well—" she shrugged "—it's a nice barn."

The tension eased for a few moments, and he couldn't help the grin that tugged at the corner of his mouth. "I'm really busy. I've got a lot to do before I fly out tomorrow afternoon."

The news seemed to startle her. "Where are you going?"

"Chicago."

"Business?"

"It's personal."

"Oh." She looked surprised, and a little hurt, as if she suspected he might be flying off to meet someone.

Some woman.

"I've got an address," he heard himself blurt. He knew what she was thinking, and while it shouldn't have mattered, it did. "By this time tomorrow night, the Ancient One will be history." He shook his head. "I'm through living like this."

She stiffened. "Is it so bad?" she finally asked after a long, silent moment. "Being a vampire?"

"Isn't it?"

"It could be worse." She shrugged. "My actual life wasn't all that great, so I guess I don't have much to compare it to."

"You could, you know." He wasn't sure why he said the words, except that she looked so sad and lonely all of a sudden, and he couldn't resist the sudden urge to ease her pain. "You could find your father and break the curse," he reminded her.

"By killing him?" She shook her head. "I could never do that." She seemed to gather her resolve. "I wouldn't do that."

"You don't owe him, Viv. Not loyalty. Not respect. Nothing."

"But I owe myself." Her gaze locked with his. "Don't you see? I can't do to him what he did to my mother. No matter how much he deserves it. That would make me no better than he was." She seemed to gather her courage. "I'm different. I am. I don't hurt people. Not on purpose. I..." Her eyes burned with desperation, and he had the sudden thought that she wanted to tell him something.

But then she seemed to think better of it. Determination lit her expression, burning up everything else, and she reached for the hem of her T-shirt instead. "We still have some unfinished business," she said. And then she pulled the cotton up and over her head.

She wasn't wearing a bra. Her bare breasts trembled as she tossed the cotton aside and reached for the drawstring on her pants. Her fingers hesitated, and he knew then that she wasn't half as confident as she pretended to be. And damned if that knowledge didn't slither across the distance to him and keep him rooted to the spot when he should have turned and hauled ass the other way.

He didn't need another test on his already tentative control.

Oh, but he wanted one. One more touch. One more kiss. One more chance to be inside of her.

She stripped completely down and stepped toward him.

Dropping to her knees in front of him, she gripped his zipper. Metal hissed, and he sprang into her hands. She trailed her fingers over him, circling the ripe, plump head of his erection.

"I wanted so much to touch you before. Too much, that's why I didn't."

He groaned. A drop of pearly liquid beaded on the head of his penis. She leaned down and closed her lips around the smooth ridge. Her fangs grazed the tender underside, and a bolt of electricity zinged through his body. Desire rushed hot on its heels. She suckled him then, and his cock throbbed in the warm heat of her mouth.

He ground his teeth together, fighting the sensation that gripped his body. He had to hold on, to hold back.

At the same time, with her mouth drawing on him and her hands tugging at his waistband, peeling the denim down his hips, it was hard to remember his objective.

Brakes, his conscience quipped. *Put on the friggin' brakes.*

He couldn't.

He pushed himself deeper into her mouth, his hands cradling her head as she sucked on him, and then he waited to see what she would do next. A long list of possibilities rushed through his head, but none of them were half as exciting as what she was doing right now.

Because it was real.

Because she was real.

Because he loved her.

Viv's last little bit of hesitation vanished when she glanced up and saw the dark desire swimming in the depths of Garret's eyes. He was following her, relishing her touch, eager for it.

She sucked him harder for several more moments before she finally pulled away and stripped the jeans completely down his legs. Then she pulled him down to the ground, urging him backwards onto the soft cushion of the hay. She climbed over him and sank down onto his hard, hot length.

Flesh met flesh as her body closed around his and ecstasy pulsed through her.

She moved, rotating her hips, her inner muscles contracting, sucking at him as the delicious pressure built inside of her.

A groan worked its way up his throat, and she saw the startled glimpse in his gaze, as if he felt everything as intensely as she did, and feared it.

When he grasped her buttocks, she thought he meant to slow her down, but he didn't.

His voice, raw and husky, echoed in her ears. "I've missed you so much." His fingers sank into her flesh. He tightened his pelvis and thrust upward at the same time that she pushed down, and it was like pure magic.

Sensation swept her up and pushed her to the edge as she sank deliciously deep. The sensation receded when she withdrew, and then hit her again when she slid back down.

Up and down.

Over and over.

Again and again.

Until pleasure crashed over her, and the most decadent orgasm flowed through her body. Along with a rush of pure joy that had nothing to do with the way his body pulsed deep inside of her and everything to do with the way he was looking at her.

His eyes blazed with passion and desire and a possessive light that said he would never, ever let her go again.

His fingers tightened on her bottom. The muscles in his arms bulged. His body went taut and a deep, husky growl rumbled from his throat.

His eyes fired even hotter, and his fangs flashed in the moonlight.

Before she could stop herself, she threw her head back and offered her neck to him.

She had the fleeting thought that he would refuse. While she truly felt something for him, she had no illusions that his feelings went any deeper than the lust that lived and breathed inside of him. No way would he want to bond himself to her.

But then his mouth closed over her neck, and his tongue stroked her pulse point. And then…he sank his fangs into her.

She'd thought the orgasm phenomenal, but it paled in comparison to the dizzying rush that crashed over her in that next instant, gripping every inch of her body.

She rode the tide of pleasure, holding tight to his shoulders as he feasted on her and heightened the sensation.

But then he pulled away, and the feelings disappeared.

He stared up at her, disbelief blazing in his eyes. Reality crashed down around her, and she knew then that her worst fear had been realized.

He'd drank from her, bonded with her, and now he knew her head. Her heart.

He knew the truth.

"You did this to me," he growled, and the betrayal in his gaze hurt far worse than the stake she'd envisioned in her dreams. "You."

19

GARRET DIDN'T PULL OUT a stake and punish Viv for turning him all those years ago.

No, what he did next was much more painful.

He pulled away from her.

"I couldn't just let you die," she said as he turned his back to her and reached for his clothes.

"It was you," he said again as if he couldn't quite believe it. But he did. She saw it in the stiffness of his body as he yanked on his pants, the tense set of his shoulders as he worked at the zipper on his jeans. Anger warred inside of him, battling with the hurt.

"I'm so sorry," she said, but he didn't so much as spare her a glance as he pulled on his boots and pushed to his feet.

She didn't blame him. She'd lied to him too many times for him to believe her now.

She'd lied to herself.

No more.

He knew the truth, and so did she.

She loved him. She always had, she'd just been too naive to realize it. Too scared. She'd been hurt so much by the people that she loved and so she hadn't wanted to love anyone.

She hadn't wanted to love him.

But she did, and so she let him walk away. Words were little solace for the pain she'd inflicted on him. An apology wasn't going to erase the past. There was only one thing that could do that.

She pulled on her clothes and headed back to town to confront Matt Keller.

If her instincts were right about him, Cruz and Molly wouldn't be far away.

"I'M SORRY."

Her soft, desperate voice echoed in Garret's head as he gunned the engine on his motorcycle and hit the dirt trail that led across the North pasture.

A rut caught the front tire, and the handlebars shook with the force of it. The custom chopper wasn't made for this and he damn well knew it, but he couldn't stop himself. He tightened his grip and opened the bike up as fast as it would go. He had to outrun the voice. The past.

The truth.

She was sorry.

He knew it as surely as he knew the sun would rise in a few hours. The knowledge sat deep down in his bones. His heart.

She hadn't wanted to turn him anymore than she'd wanted to turn all the others in her past. He'd seen their faces when he'd drank from her—faces that haunted her dreams and refused her any peace—and he'd felt her remorse.

The bike jumped, startling him as much as the regret now swimming inside of him. Her regret.

For ruining so many lives. For betraying him.

She hadn't meant to.

Rather, she'd saved him because she hadn't been able to bear losing him. And then she'd turned her back on him because she hadn't been able to bear his hatred should he discover the truth.

Because she loved him.

Then and now.

Always.

The realization sent a burst of pure happiness through him, followed by a rush of dread. He gunned the engine faster, pushing the bike as fast and as far as it would go. Because maybe, just maybe if he burned up the engine he could escape the inevitable that beat at his temples.

Viv was the vampire. The one he and Jake and Dillon had been searching for all these months. The key to his humanity. The answer to his desperate prayers.

The Ancient One.

And she had to die.

It was the only way to free all of them. To free himself. He was tired of being a slave to the beast inside. He wanted to be normal again. To laugh. To love. To be whole.

He slammed on the brakes and skidded to a stop. The transmission screamed as he swerved the bike in a one-eighty and shifted into gear. And then he did what he should have done in the first place—he headed for town.

It was time to reclaim his humanity.

"WHERE ARE THEY?" Viv demanded when Sheriff Matt Keller hauled open the motel room door after her second knock.

"Do you know what time it is?" He wiped at his tired-looking face and glared at her.

"Cruz and Molly. You know them, right?" She pushed her way into his room and kicked the door shut. Her gaze sliced through the darkness, touching every corner as if she expected the duo of vampires to pop out at her.

Or rather, she hoped. Then it would all be over and the pain twisting at her heart would end.

"You led them to me in Washington, and you're leading them to me now," she told him. "Where are they? Just tell me, and I'll go to them. I'm tired of waiting. I want this over with."

He flipped on a nearby light. The small bulb pushed back the shadows to reveal a worn duffel bag sitting next to the bed. His badge and gun lay on the nightstand next to a half empty bottle of soda. He eyed her. "Have you been drinking?"

"I know you know where they are. Tell me."

"I don't have a friggin' clue what you're talking about, lady, but I'll make sure to add 'crazy' to the other list of offenses on your rap sheet."

"I know you didn't come here just to get my notes

on the Butcher. You're working for Cruz and Molly. What are you? A blood slave?" That would explain why she hadn't been able to read him. If he were feeding one of the vampires, they would have control over him. They could block his thoughts. They could wipe his mind clean until he was little more than a zombie.

But they couldn't make his eyes glow.

She watched as the green depths magnified, growing brighter and more intense.

"What are you?" she asked again. As much as she was hoping for the blood slave explanation, she had a gut feeling she wasn't even close.

"I should be asking you that question." He stepped closer then. "I know you're not human. I can feel it." His tall body loomed over her, backing her up a few steps.

Insane, right? She was a big, bad vampire.

But Matt Keller seemed just as dangerous. Strength rolled off him, along with a feral air that stalled her heartbeat and made her wonder if he didn't intend to save Cruz and Molly the trouble and kill her himself.

"You're like me, aren't you?" he demanded. Before she could respond, he continued, "You are. You have to be. You're too strong to be human. Too different." His gaze grew brighter, hotter and his mouth opened. She saw the teeth then. Not just a pair of fangs, but two full rows of them. A growl vibrated up his throat. A wildness lit his eyes and carved his expression. Reality dawned.

"You're a werewolf?" It had been hard enough accepting the truth of what she'd become, and she'd lived every painful moment of the change. Denial pumped through her. There had to be another explanation. "I don't believe this. There's no such thing."

His lips pulled back and he growled, a strange, inhuman sound that slid into her ears and chased away all doubt.

"Oh, my God."

"God didn't have anything to do with it." His expression relaxed, and the savage air that had gripped him seemed to ease. The muscles in his face shifted, his bones pushing and pulling until the familiar face of Sheriff Matt Keller stared back at her. "It's genetic, at least that's what my father told me. And it's rare."

"I hate to break this to you, but I don't howl at the full moon." When he gave her a sharp look, she added, "Not that your instincts were wrong. I'm not human, but I'm not a werewolf, either. I'm a vampire."

He looked at her as if she'd just confessed to giving birth to the three-headed alien in Oregon. "There's no such thing."

This from the Wolf Man? "Listen, buddy, if werewolves can exist, so can vampires."

"Werewolves don't exist. Just one. Me." He looked so alone in that next instant that she could actually understand why he'd come all the way from Washington. "I'm all that's left since my folks died. That's why I was so determined to find you. I thought maybe... Finally..." He shook his head and eyed her. "You're sure you're not a werewolf?"

"Trust me." To prove her point, she flashed him her fangs. She went on to tell him the short version of her life story—namely that she was being hunted by two vamps determined to destroy her. She finished with "That's why I barged in just now. I thought you knew them. I'm really sorry." She glanced at the rumpled sheets. "I didn't mean to wake you."

"I couldn't sleep anyway." He eyed the open window. Beyond, the moon hung huge and round, and his eyes glowed for a split-second. "It's two days until the moon is at its fullest. I'm supposed to mate then. At least, I think I am. But then, I've never actually done it because there are no female werewolves around. Which means I end up with a human female." He shook his head. "It's not the same. Not that I actually know, I just feel it. I keep thinking there ought to be more excitement to it. More oomph…" He let his voice trail off as if he'd already said too much. "I don't mean to dump all of this on you. I just don't get a chance to talk about it much. Don't sweat the barging in. I never really sleep much, especially this time of the month. I've tried pills, warm milk, the works, but nothing helps."

"Do you really howl at the moon?"

"Do you really suck blood?"

"Point made." She grinned and he grinned and despite the fact that he was a werewolf and she was a vampire, she actually felt a sort of camaraderie. Not the same connection she felt with Garret, of course. That was deeper, more profound.

But this… This was nice.

Suddenly, she could understand why Garret was so anxious to find and kill the vampire that turned him.

He wasn't just doing it for himself.

He was doing it for his friends.

At least, he wanted to. But he wouldn't get the chance because Cruz and Molly were about to beat him to it.

She knew it the moment the hair on the back of her neck stood on end. Awareness raced down her spine. Every muscle in her body went tight. The door crashed open behind her.

Viv whirled in time to see Cruz lunging for her, a stake in his hand and murder on his mind.

20

VIV DIDN'T MOVE as the vampire lunged. Instead, she closed her eyes and braced herself for the pain.

But instead of feeling the sharp stab of the stake, she felt Matt Keller's hand on her arm.

"Run," he told her as he shoved her out of the way. The stake caught him in the shoulder, and a loud howl filled the room.

His eyes glowed, and he reached for Cruz, his hands going for the vampire's throat. Before his fingers could make contact, Molly flew into the room.

"No!" Viv cried, but the female vampire had already caught Keller and jerked him backwards. Her fangs sank into his neck.

She lunged to her feet and rushed forward, but Cruz caught her by the hair.

"You're going to die this time," he spat as he yanked her around and shoved her back up against the wall.

Her head smashed into the sheetrock. Pain split open her skull, and her gut clenched. Anger rolled through her, along with the need for survival.

Live, the beast chanted. *Fight. Destroy.*

"Do it," she ground out. It was too late to save Keller, but it wasn't too late to save everyone else. "Just go ahead and do it."

He raised the stake high into the air and she closed her eyes.

"No!" Garret's voice pushed past the frantic beat of her heart. Her eyes snapped open in time to see him catch the stake mid-air.

Cruz turned on him, his gaze flashing red fury as he lunged at Garret.

Viv moved forward to help, but Molly tackled her. She hit the wall again, and chunks of plaster flew. Blood dripped from the woman's mouth and streamed down her neck as she gripped Viv by the collar and threw her against the opposite wall.

Her vision blurred from the impact, but a loud wail yanked her back to the present.

Viv scrambled to her feet just as Garret sank the stake into the crazed vampire's chest.

Cruz stumbled backwards, a surprised look on his face. He teetered and then he collapsed.

"Molly." The name tumbled from his lips and then his body went deathly still.

"Baby?" Molly crumbled to the floor next to Cruz and touched his face. "Come on. Open your eyes," she begged. "Don't do this to me. It's you and me. Together. Forever. Remember?" She shook her head frantically as she touched his chest. Her hand closed around the stake. "Forever." She pulled the stake free.

Just when Viv thought she meant to turn it on herself, she whirled. She flew at Viv, but Garret caught her.

He anchored one hand around her waist and reached for the stake with his other. He was an older vampire and, therefore, stronger. She soon went slack in his grasp.

"I'm only going to say this once." He tossed her to the ground and held up the stake. "You can end up like your friend there, or you can get the hell out. It's your choice, and you'd better make it fast. Before I change my mind."

"Kiss my ass." Molly lunged at him, in full attack mode.

Viv tackled her, sending her sideways. They both crashed into the door. She grabbed Molly's hair and hung on, fighting to keep her down and away from Garret.

She didn't have to fight long. One minute she was staring up at Molly, holding her at arm's length, and the next, the woman went rigid.

Molly gasped, and blood spurted from her mouth as she pitched forward. Viv rolled out from under her, and that's when she saw the sharp piece of the wooden doorframe that protruded from between her shoulder blades.

Garret stood just inches away, his eyes blazing with a protective light and something else. Something that stalled her heartbeat.

"Are you okay?"

"You saved me," she said accusingly. "Why?"

Because I love you.

That's what his gaze said, but she didn't just want to see it. She needed to hear it.

Before she could open her mouth again, a groan carried from the far corner. She turned just as Matt Keller staggered to his feet. Blood still gushed from his neck, and he looked dangerously pale, but already the wound had started to close.

"Don't tell me. Werewolves have rejuvenating capabilities."

"You know it." He staggered back a few steps and collapsed on the edge of the bed.

"Maybe you should lie down." Viv reached him in the blink of an eye and urged him back down. She checked the wound, and sure enough, the skin had already started to knit back together. "I know how this goes for vampires. A little sleep, and we're fine."

He nodded. "Sleep is good."

"Do you need anything?"

"Just some peace and quiet."

Viv nodded and turned to Garret. "We'd better get them out of here." She motioned to Molly and Cruz. They were still intact, but come sunup, their bodies would start to disintegrate.

Garret nodded, and they spent the next half hour moving the bodies out to his barn. Once they finished, she turned on him.

She'd waited long enough for the truth.

"You never answered my question. Why did you face off with Cruz? You should have been helping him."

"I won't let you die."

"You don't get to make that decision. My father beat you to it."

"No, he didn't." He shook his head. "He took your humanity, but he didn't take your soul, Viv. You're still a good person. You weren't trying to hurt Cruz and Molly. You helped them. You did what they asked of you."

"You never asked."

"I would have. If I had known what you were, I would have. For the chance to be with you again, to touch you, to kiss you, to talk to you, I would have begged."

"What are you saying?"

"That I love you. I've always loved you."

"Because I was a vampire."

"I loved you then—I love you now—in spite of the fact that you're a vampire. And I won't let you sacrifice yourself. You didn't set out to hurt anyone. You did what you thought was right."

"But—"

"There is no but." Certainty gleamed in his eyes, along with a brilliant light that filled her with a burst of warmth. Because he did love her, and he meant every word he said.

"You gave them all a chance to right their wrongs," he went on. "A chance to live. To love. If they didn't want that, if the hunger led them down the wrong path, that's their problem. You don't owe anyone."

But Garret did.

Jake. Dillon. While he hadn't initially attacked them

on purpose, they were his friends. They'd been his friends even though he'd doomed them. They'd stood by him, waiting patiently, searching for the Ancient One.

For Viv.

He wouldn't give her up.

At the same time, he couldn't let his friends down. He'd been content as a vampire until he'd gotten to know Jake. Jake had forced him to remember the man he'd once been, to miss his humanity, because Jake missed his.

Garret saw the truth when he looked at Jake and Nikki. They wanted so much to be together. To be normal. And they were depending on Garret to make it happen.

But Garret couldn't sacrifice the woman he loved—he wouldn't. Tonight had proved as much. They were bonded now. She was his, now and always, and he would defend her until the last dying beat of his heart.

No, he wouldn't sacrifice Viv so that his friends could walk in the sunlight.

He wouldn't have to.

He'd been the one to take Jake's humanity from him, and he could give it back.

"No." Viv shook her head. "You're not going to—"

He pressed a fingertip to her lips. "No more talk. I need to be inside of you tonight."

Their last night.

Because Garret was through living with the guilt and the regret. He owed Jake, and it was time to ante up.

He scooped Viv into his arms and headed for the main house.

21

HE CARRIED HER into the house and down the steps into the basement.

His room. She knew it as she stared at the large area with its open rafters and king-size bed.

He dropped her to her feet, flipped on a light switch and then turned back to her. His gaze burned with an intensity that made her body tremble.

She knew what he was going to do.

Not because she read it in his thoughts. Despite the fact that they were bonded, she still couldn't see inside his head because he'd put up a mental wall to shut her out.

No, she felt the truth in the urgent way he touched her, kissed her, as if he wanted to brand this moment into his memory.

She forced her mouth from his. "You can't—" she started, but then he kissed her again, silencing her words.

She slid her arms around him and held him tight, refusing to let go. Not now as he made love to her, and not afterward.

Not ever.

She drew a ragged breath when he tore his mouth from hers to leave a fiery trail down the length of her neck to the hollow between her breasts. Then he released her, his hands going to the buttons of her blouse, his movements urgent as if they had not a moment to spare.

He pushed the edges open and unhooked her bra, baring her aching breasts. Dipping his head, he closed his mouth over one swollen nipple and greedily sucked the sensitive flesh.

She matched his urgency with her own as her hands found the waistband of his jeans. She heard the groan that rumbled from his throat as she trailed her fingers over the bulge of the material. Impatiently she tugged at the zipper and dipped her hands inside.

Hot and hard, his shaft pulsed, swelling even more when she brushed her fingers along its silky length.

He lifted his head and captured her with his heated gaze, stoking the fire already raging inside her. She kissed the pulse at the base of his neck, her hands moving up and down his arousal. She rained kisses over his chest, laving his nipples with her tongue.

His arms wrapped tight around her as he pulled her even closer. "I need to feel your heat around me, your sweet fangs in my neck," he said, his lips a soft vibration on hers.

Then he kissed her again, plunging his tongue inside to explore and savor. He grazed the very tip of one fang, and she felt the stroke between her legs.

When he moved his mouth to leave a burning path

down her neck, she tilted back her head, pleasure rushing to her brain and building the anticipation. His tongue traced the slope of her breast, down around its fullness, and a cry tore from her lips the moment he found her nipple again.

Viv buried her hands in his hair, holding him close, arching her breast into the moistness of his mouth. His fangs were sharp, prickling her soft skin but not biting her. No, he wanted what she'd held back from him the last time.

He sucked, and she felt the waves of heat build inside her, rising higher like molten lava in a volcano, until she felt ready to erupt.

She wouldn't. Not yet. Not until they were really and truly one.

In one swift motion, he unzipped her jeans and pushed them down, making quick work of his own. Then he locked her in his powerful arms and lifted her.

She clung to him, wrapping her legs around him as he slid her down onto his rigid length, the delicious friction sending jolts of electricity shooting through her body, singeing every nerve until she burned as hot as the man inside her.

She didn't know when he moved them. She only felt the bed against her back, the pulsing heat between her legs. Lifting her hips, she grasped his muscled buttocks and pulled him closer, deeper, her desire for him overriding all else.

She rose to meet each fierce thrust, taking all that he could give and wanting more.

So much more.

They came together in a frenzied, primitive act. Hunger made them burn, desperation a potent aphrodisiac that heightened their senses and stirred their appetite.

She reached for him, pulling him down as she felt the first waves of pleasure begin. The beast rose inside of her, and she didn't fight it this time. Need rushed through her, and her entire body went tight. A hiss worked its way up her throat, and she drew back her lips.

His pulse pounded against her tongue, begging her to sink her fangs deep, but she couldn't bring herself to take his blood. She'd taken far too much from him already.

"You didn't take." His voice was gruff against the shell of her ear. "You gave. You wanted me to live and so you gave me back the life that those bandits took from me. You don't owe me anything, baby. I owe you." His fingers splayed at the base of her head, and he pulled her closer, pressing her fangs against his neck until they sank deep.

His sweet essence filled her mouth, and a burst of electricity sizzled across her nerve endings.

"Drink," he urged, and she couldn't stop herself.

She drew him in, relishing the missile of heat that spread through her body and firebombed between her legs.

She sucked harder, faster, feasting at his neck the way her body feasted on his rock-hard erection.

Arching her body, she pulled him in even deeper. He growled and bucked and spilled himself deep inside.

She held on to him as he gave himself to her. His blood. His body. His soul.

The realization hit her, and she forced her mouth away. She stared up at him and saw the emotion blazing in his eyes.

Even more, she felt it in the way he covered her mouth with his own and kissed her. Slowly. Tenderly.

He loved her.

And she loved him.

And for the next few moments, the world seemed to fall away as she clung to him and he held her tight.

"I'm not letting you go," she murmured against his neck, her voice thick with conviction.

She'd been powerless to save her mother all those years ago, but she wasn't powerless now. And she wasn't going to turn her back and walk away from him again.

She would beg. She would plead. And he would listen. He wouldn't leave her.

He wouldn't.

That's what she told herself. But as the minutes slipped by and dawn approached, she couldn't shake the sinking feeling that in his head, in his heart, he was already gone.

HE WAS SOUND ASLEEP.

Viv stood next to the bed and stared down at Garret's muscular body sprawled across the white sheets. He lay on his stomach, his arm still stretched out beside him, covering the indentation her body had made.

He hadn't budged when she'd slipped from the bed, despite the fact that it was still dark outside and he should be at the peak of his strength right now, particularly since they'd just had sex.

But as much energy as she'd given, she'd taken in return by drinking from him, and so he was wiped out. He needed at least an hour or two of sleep to regain his strength.

Then he would climb from the bed and do the unthinkable.

If she didn't do something first.

She touched the smooth sinewy skin of one shoulder and pressed a soft kiss against his temple.

And then Viv pulled on her clothes, grabbed her purse and went to save Garret Sawyer from himself.

IT WAS ALMOST FIVE in the morning, and everything in town had long since closed up shop for the night. The streets were dark and shadowed as Viv drove the short distance to Skull Creek Choppers. The small neon sign blazed in the window. Her senses went into overload, buzzing and humming from being so close to the two vampires inside.

She pulled into the back parking lot, killed her engine and climbed from the front seat. The door was locked, and she knocked. Doubt crawled up and down her spine as she waited for someone to answer. She almost called it quits.

Almost.

But she loved Garret too much to let him sacrifice

so much for her. She knew he was trying to save her, and she wasn't going to let him. Not again.

She was through taking from Garret. It was time for her to give back.

The door opened, and she found herself staring at a tall, handsome vampire. He had long dark hair, blue eyes and a puzzled expression.

"Jake McCann?" she asked, and he nodded.

"My name is Viviana Darland. I have something you want, and I need to give it back." And then she walked into Skull Creek Choppers, spilled her guts about the past and the future and what was going to happen if Jake didn't pop a stake into her right here and now.

And then she waited for him to take the decision out of Garret's hands and put them all out of their misery.

22

GARRET PARKED HIS pick-up near the gate of the eastern pasture and climbed out. A quick leap, and he stood on the other side of the fence where he kept the bucking horses. They were spread out. One stood in the far corner chewing on a hay bale. A few others had galloped over the ridge when they'd heard his pick-up. Only Delilah stood nearby, munching on the remains of one of the hay bales he'd dropped off earlier that week.

"Easy, girl. I'm not here to bother you." Garret held up his hands. "Not this time."

She danced backwards a few steps and eyed him, her eyes wide, fearful, as if she didn't trust him.

She didn't, and she never would, and it didn't matter anymore. Because Viviana Darland loved him.

The truth sang through his head and relaxed his tight muscles. She'd loved him as a man, and she loved him as a vampire and that emotion filled the emptiness that had haunted him for so long.

He realized now that all of the desperate attempts to reclaim his humanity hadn't been because he'd missed what he'd once been…but because he'd hated what he'd become. Restless. Lonely. Empty. He hadn't wanted to be a man again half as much as he'd wanted to feel whole.

The way he'd felt during those few weeks when he'd been with Viv.

But then she'd walked away.

That's what had destroyed him. Not losing his humanity, but losing her. He hadn't spent the past century regretting what he'd become. Other than not being able to tell his folks goodbye, he'd actually been content being a vampire. Sure, he wasn't too keen on the yearly turning, but he'd learned how to control it, with the exception of Jake and Dillon. And while he regretted biting them, he couldn't regret the bond they'd forged.

They were his friends.

His family.

No, he'd come to appreciate the perks of being a vampire. He liked being strong. Reading minds. Being great in bed.

Until he'd watched Jake fall in love with Nikki. Then he'd remembered what it was like to be in love himself—really and truly in love—and he'd missed it.

He'd missed Viv.

She'd come back to him now and given him the most precious gift of all—her love—and he owed her.

His love.

His protection.

He'd already eliminated the vampires threatening her existence. All except for one.

Jake had fought too hard, too long to simply give up the search for his humanity now, not with Nikki still human. Sure, they could go after Viv's father, but he could be halfway around the world for all they knew. They had no clues. And even if they did manage to track him down, Viv would never let them destroy him.

She would sacrifice herself first to save all of them, if for no other reason than to prove that she wasn't like the man who'd made her childhood a living hell.

Vampire or not, she would never willingly hurt anyone.

He knew that now. He knew her.

Her head.

Her heart.

He also knew that he would do anything in his power to keep her safe.

He'd eliminated the two vampires who'd threatened her existence, and now it was time to take care of the last and final threat.

He walked several more feet until he reached a far tree near the edge of the pasture. It was the same tree he'd camped out at that night so long ago when he'd been attacked and left to die.

Viv had saved him, and now it was his turn to repay the favor. He would give Jake and Dillon their humanity back, and the hunt for the Ancient One would end right now.

Sitting down, he leaned back against the tree, his legs stretched out in front of him.

And then he fixed his gaze on the eastern horizon and waited for the sun to rise.

"GARRET." THE NAME whispered on the wind, and Garret thought for a split-second that it was his imagination. Until he felt a nudge against his leg.

He opened his eyes to see Jake standing in front of him. Orange tinged the horizon behind him, and a faint stream of smoke whispered around the vampire. It was almost time now. He could feel it in the lull of his muscles and the weariness that pulled at his eyelids. They drifted shut again, and he felt the nudge of a boot against his leg.

"You stupid sonofabitch." It was Jake's voice again, pulling him from the exhaustion and the dream he was having.

He and Viv were together. She loved him and he loved her and all was right with the world.

"Come on. Get up." Jake's voice grew stronger, reminding Garret that it was just his wishful thinking.

Nothing was right and there would be no happily ever after. Not for him.

But that was okay. She would be safe. Alive.

"Leave me alone," he told Jake when the vampire nudged him again.

"And let you fry for some woman? What the hell is wrong with you?"

He opened his eyes then and stared up at his friend. "She's the Ancient One." He shook his head. "This is the only way."

"Do you love her?" Jake demanded.

"What does that have to do with anything?"

"Do you?"

"I've always loved her."

"Then forget this self-sacrifice crap, get the hell up and do something about it."

"But you and Dillon—"

"—aren't going to last two days without your sorry ass to boss us around." Jake hunkered down in front of Garret. "We need you, man."

"You need your humanity."

"I always thought so." Jake shook his head. "I thought if I could just go back and erase the past hundred or so years, then I would feel different. I would feel hopeful, optimistic, free. I've spent so long being a slave to the hunger, and I just wanted to be free. But then I found Nikki."

"And you wanted it even more."

"Only because I thought it was what she wanted. But she loves me, even if I never become human again. She loves me just the way I am. And she'll keep loving me, for a lifetime or an eternity. Meg feels the same about Dillon." His gaze caught and held Garret's. "And Viv feels the same about you. She loves you, man. Don't blow this." He pushed to his feet. "Get your ass up, and let me take you home."

But Garret couldn't because he knew what Jake was thinking. They would just go after Viv's sire.

"I know about her father," Jake said, as if reading Garret's thoughts. "She told me."

"You talked to her?"

"She came to me and offered herself. She wanted to take the decision away from you. So she told me who she was, and then asked me to kill her." Before Garret could move, Jake held up a hand. "Calm down. I didn't touch her."

"Why not?"

"For the same reason that you're sitting here right now, ready to fry. We're friends, Garret. Now and always. If you love her, that's good enough for me."

"And me." Dillon stepped up behind Jake.

"Ditto for me." It was Nikki's turn. She slid an arm around Jake's waist.

"And me," added Meg as she came up beside Dillon.

"But it's not good enough for me." Viv's sweet voice slid into his ears, and he watched as she stepped from behind the group and walked over to him.

He pushed to his feet then, despite the fatigue that bound his muscles. Suddenly, he didn't feel half as drained as he had a few minutes ago. Not with Viv here. Now.

She fed his strength in a way that went way beyond blood and sex. She fed his soul. With her smiles and her laughter.

"I want more than your love," she told him as she stopped just inches away, determination etching her beautiful features. "I want to fall asleep in your arms and wake up to you every evening. I want you. Every moment of every day. Every day from now until forever. You." She touched him, her fingertips brushing his jaw as she reached out. Her eyes glimmered with emotion and his chest tightened. "Please don't do this."

Garret sighed. It looked as if he had no choice, even if he'd wanted it. And he didn't. "Then we all agree it stops here." He glanced around the small group. "No more searching for the Ancient One. It's over right here and now."

"Right here," Jake added.

"Right now," came Dillon's solemn agreement.

"Besides, I hear that fangs are the new thing this year," Nikki added.

"It's what all of Skull Creek's finest are wearing," said Meg.

Garret grinned and turned back to Viv. His expression faded as he stared at the woman he loved. The vampire he'd always loved.

"Let's get the hell out of here," he murmured. And then he pulled her into his arms and held on tight.

Epilogue

His HEAD HURT like a sonofabitch.

Sheriff Matt Keller forced his eyes open to the blinding morning sunlight that pushed past the drapes. He rolled over onto his back and winced against the pain that beat at his temples.

He felt as if he'd drank the night away and passed out in an alley somewhere. His entire body felt stiff, his muscles tight. A groan worked its way up his throat as he pushed into a sitting position.

He blinked and focused on his surroundings.

And then he blinked again because nothing was the way he remembered when he'd first crawled between the sheets last night.

The door hung from one hinge, and every piece of furniture except the bed had been smashed to bits. There was a sizeable dent in one wall and a litter of sheetrock on the floor. It looked as if Godzilla had faced off with King Kong, and neither had won.

What the hell…?

He closed his eyes and tried to remember. He'd checked the parking lot for Viv Darland's car one more time, then he'd crawled into bed and flipped on the TV to pass the time and wait for her to come in. He'd wanted to talk to her. To get her to confess.

He'd done just that, but only after she'd come knocking on his door. He remembered her accusations, her revelation. The attack.

Holy shit.

He'd been bitten by a vampire.

As if he didn't have enough friggin' problems of his own.

He touched a hand to his neck, but the wound had already healed thanks to his werewolf DNA. The only lingering reminders of last night were the very real images in his head and the Metallica solo that pounded in his head.

Oh, and the little old woman standing in the doorway. Towels overflowed her arms and a disapproving expression etched her face.

She eyed the surrounding mess and arched one eyebrow. "I hope you know this means you ain't getting your deposit back."

He shrugged. "I sort of figured."

She took another look before her gaze zeroed in on him again and dropped to his lap. "You always sleep in your birthday suit?"

He glanced down and sure enough, he was bucknaked. "I like to be comfortable."

"Me, too. Say, you're not a bad-looking fella. If you're interested in a date, I might be able to help you out."

"Thanks, but I'll pass."

"Let me know if you change your mind. There's lots of pretty girls around here."

His body seemed to come alive just at the thought. His gut tightened and his groin stirred. He snatched up a nearby pillow just before the old woman got an eyeful.

"I've got a really busy job. Maybe next time."

"Suit yourself." She shrugged and waddled past his doorway, her orthopedic shoes slapping the pavement outside.

He moved the pillow and stared down at his lap. At the monster that had once been his penis. He'd never been short on equipment. He was a werewolf, after all, which meant he had the whole survival of the fittest thing going on—primitive alpha male, leader of the pack, the whole nine yards.

But this…

This gave new meaning to the word "enormous" and made him wonder what other not-so-little changes lay in store for him now that he'd been bitten by a vampire.

Only time would tell.

* * * * *

Wait! The story's not over yet.
What happens when a werewolf
gets bitten by a vampire?
Find out in ONCE UPON A BITE by Kimberly Raye,
the first novella in Blazing Bedtime Stories,
Blaze's 2009 Valentine Collection.
Don't miss it!

Silhouette®

SPECIAL EDITION™

FROM *NEW YORK TIMES* BESTSELLING AUTHOR

LINDA LAEL MILLER

A STONE CREEK CHRISTMAS

Veterinarian Olivia O'Ballivan finds the animals in Stone Creek playing Cupid between her and Tanner Quinn. Even Tanner's daughter, Sophie, is eager to play matchmaker. With everyone conspiring against them and the holiday season fast approaching, Tanner and Olivia may just get everything they want for Christmas after all!

Available December 2008
wherever books are sold.

nocturne™

New York Times bestselling author

MERLINE LOVELACE

LORI DEVOTI

HOLIDAY WITH A VAMPIRE II

**CELEBRATE THE HOLIDAYS WITH TWO
BREATHTAKING STORIES FROM
NEW YORK TIMES BESTSELLING AUTHOR
MERLINE LOVELACE AND LORI DEVOTI.**

Two vampires, each wary of human relationships,
are put to the test when holiday encounters blur
the boundaries of passion and hunger.

Available December wherever books are sold.

REQUEST YOUR FREE BOOKS!

2 FREE NOVELS
PLUS 2
FREE GIFTS!

HARLEQUIN®

Blaze™

Red-hot reads!

HB08R

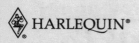

HOLLY JACOBS
Once Upon a Christmas

Daniel McLean is thrilled to learn he
may be the father of Michelle Hamilton's
nephew. When Daniel starts to spend
time with Brandon and help her organize
Erie Elementary's big Christmas Fair, the
three discover a paternity test won't make
them a family, but the love they discover
just might....

***Available December 2008
wherever books are sold.***

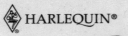

HARLEQUIN®

COMING NEXT MONTH

#435 HEATING UP THE HOLIDAYS
Jill Shalvis, Jacquie D'Alessandro, Jamie Sobrato
A Hunky Holiday Collection
Santa's finally figured out what women want—hot guys! And these three lucky ladies unwrap three of the hottest men around. Don't miss this Christmas anthology, guaranteed to live up to its title!

#436 YULE BE MINE Jennifer LaBrecque
Forbidden Fantasies
Journalist Giselle Randolph is looking forward to her upcoming assignment in Sedona…until she learns that her photographer is Sam McKendrick—the man she's lusted after for most of her life, the man she used to call her brother.…

#437 COME TOY WITH ME Cara Summers
Navy captain Dino Angelis might share a bit of his family's "sight," but even he never dreamed he'd be spending the holidays playing protector to sexy toy-store owner Cat McGuire. Or that he'd be fighting his desire to play with her himself…

#438 WHO NEEDS MISTLETOE? Kate Hoffmann
24 Hours: Lost, Bk. 1
Sophie Madigan hadn't intended to spend Christmas Eve flying rich boy Trey Shelton III around the South Pacific…or to make a crash landing. Still, now that she's got seriously sexy Trey all to herself for twenty-four hours, why not make it a Christmas to remember?

#439 RESTLESS Tori Carrington
Indecent Proposals, Bk. 2
Lawyer Lizzie Gilbred has always been a little too proper…until she meets hot guitarist Patrick Gauge. But even mind-blowing sex may not be enough for Lizzie to permanently let down her guard—or for Gauge to stick around.…

#440 NO PEEKING… Stephanie Bond
Sex for Beginners, Bk. 3
An old letter reminds Violet Summerlin that she'd dreamed about sex that was exciting, all-consuming, *dangerous!* And dreams were all they were…until her letter finds its way to sexy Dominick Burns…

www.eHarlequin.com

HBCNM1108